Microcosmic Girl AND THE Dracon Shapeshifter

ROY PETERS

AuthorHouse™ UK
1663 Liberty Drive
Bloomington, IN 47403 USA
www.authorhouse.co.uk
UK TFN: 0800 0148641 (Toll Free inside the UK)
UK Local: 02036 956322 (+44 20 3695 6322 from outside the UK)

This book is printed on acid-free paper.

ISBN: 979-8-8230-8817-6 (sc)
ISBN: 979-8-8230-8818-3 (e)

Print information available on the last page.

Published by AuthorHouse 06/11/2024

authorHOUSE®

CHAPTER ONE

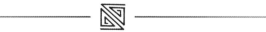

THE OFFICE BLOCK INFERNO

It was as Abigail fryler she wakes up from her bed in the middle of the night hearing sirens from the emganncey services and after having a nightmarish dream.

So she punches the wall in anger as in her mind she sees a lizard woman in mid-flight with wings blowing flames from her mouth.

So she has an itching sensation in her arms and legs her adopted mother pam puts down to her eating biscuits in the bed and also cakes.

As in arcaarting bed bugs.

As her room has a few biscuit wrappers in the bin of which is full and also she picks up the comic of her aisle self from another universes as Micrcsomic girl.

So she looks at it and heads to her wardrobe and puts

On her superhero costume that is to kind a try on type with navy blouse, yellow kitchen washing up gloves with swimming goggles and a pair of jeans she has one.

So she wonders how comes a beaded eloercnal necklace is hanging in her wardrobe on a hanger and it happens to have medallion of plastic cd like stand by button.

So the Nosie of the sirens make her anger due to what she sees in her mind and also as she puts on the TV on sky

So she then sneaks outside and then all of a sudden she leaps out into the air and flies without wings to wear she sees an office block on fire in Euston central west London.

So fly's away from where she lives with her posted parents at the house live in bloomford road, media vale, at number 23a in a cull de sac.

So she fly's upwards in the moonlit sky and fly's to the scene of the office block on fire and then sees a lizard woman with wings devoting flames from her mouth at the office block headquarters of maycourt investment holdings plc.

So the top eight floors are aloha on flames cases by the lizard dragon woman none as dryacon as she shape shifts in mid-flight with police marksmen firing bullets from their guns so they get diecesrted as Micrcsomic girl fly's towards the flying lizard woman wo tuts and grins at the young superhero girl.

'ha ha so you want stop me from burning this buldiing also scrcing into rubble and also the rest of the earth'

Says the lizard woman whip flaps her wings and stands next to Micrcsomic girl in mid-flight.

So then Micrcsomic girl folds her arms and then clinches her just as the lizard woman turns her tension at the police marksmen blow down in Euston square.

So then she blows fires flames from her mouth at first targets the gun marksmen then open traffic in Euston road like the buses, cars and taxies.

So then four of the marketmen are hit by the flames.

So then three double deck number 27 London buses are hit flames from the lizard woman.

So then cries of help are herd in the office tower block with top six floors fire with flames seeding to the lower floors.

So then Micrcsomic girl uses her freeze rays from her breath to cool the flames and then confronts the lizard woman who fly's to the roof top as two RAF fight planes fire missiles at the reptile woman.

So she does the missiles and it hits a lorry In Euston road and the then street and area surrounding Euston looks like a war zone and news networks televise the indent none as reptile Dryacon terrow attack.

So as she fly's to the top of the roof microsomal girl as the flames are stumped by water out also by the fire brigade officers in a haziest in a hoist crane.

So then with the temperature being very hot the glass sheeters form the lower floors with broken glass all over the emganncey crew below.

CHAPTER TWO

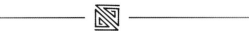

THE FAILED TRAP TO CAPTURE SHE TORE

So as microcosmic girl sours to the roof top she sees a blonde woman in a red dress sacking and crying with tears in her eyes.

She Micrcsomic girl does not see the is changing a reptile shape shifter in human adult female form.

So the woman with the red drees stands at the edge of roof floor attempting to jump of the roof.

So then somehow the superhero girl alliiase Abigail fryler transforms form her superhero girl self as Micrcsomic girl back as Abigail fryler as she speaks to the women in the red dress.

'Places don't jumbo as it can't be that bad as I can help you by not jumping'

So the woman turns over and sees Abigail with ripped jeans on her knew area of her jeans and a blue t-shirt

So then the woman with red dress cunningly at first smiles and then Abigail frlyer

Transmutes into her superhero self as microsmic girl in front of the woman who calls herself Rachel miller as Abigail asks wants to know her name.

. So you are very young to be as a superhero as I have powers in my mind I can't control what are you none as young superhero girl'

So the superhero girl grins and sighs and is interrupted as Abigail fryler calls herself

'Well in a microcosmic superhero and not none globally yet'

'You are a microcosmic girl I suppose'

.yeah and I have to get home once I find were that hurried winged reptile woman is'

Says Abigail who stops the woman with red drees from falling of the roof of office block of which is on fire.

So then all of in a minute the woman with red dress shape shifts into a reptile adult female with wings.

So she sours down and drops a metal translation ball on the ground and smashes and Micrcsomic girl sees it shattering into pieces and then she uses her powers to moulid the glass blue bowl back together.

So police marketmen hold their fire by calling ceasefire from the commanding officer in charge as microcosm girl hands the moulded tight glass bowl to the senior officer none a chief commander knit roche.

'oh one you I supped and what is it you want me and my officers to do with this as it's not play time young superhero girl and have not you got school to go to later in the morning'

'it's device that can track her where she is and I am sure she will go looking for it as she is a tingling of the reptile kind and I had dreams of her'

So the senior officers scoffe with laugher at her and one of the young pc men at the police station were there I braced of blue police tape stop plea from walking to the carnage of the scene of the crime.

So then police officer with red hair sally says

'So and pigs will fly'

So then in the sky above on this moonlit sky with the asp the light potion of which they notice the reptile female adult flying towards them and put take out there sedative dart guns pellets into the weapons as the officers are told by the commander to fire the sedate pellets at the repel or tazer taper at the woman..

So they lay the crystal ball on the pavement next to the police cordon were marketmen hold takers and sedative Pell kit guns at the reptile adult female.

So as she gets closer they lance an enactment net of metal wire mess at her but fail as she picks up the crystal ball and fly's upwards and taunts the offers and also microcosmic girl.

'ha ha me shetore I can never be beaten as I am destroy of worlds and of humans like you lot ha ha'

Yells out loud the lizard woman none shetore.

So then the comading officer tells his men to fire at will and then stop as microsmic girl attempts to stop the lizard woman.

As the both of them bark three from meatal wire mesh and then the lizard flied of into sky.

So then the offers decide not to fire at the superhero girl any to a few as microcosmic girl.

CHAPTER THREE

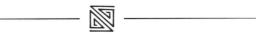

THE TRANSMUTATION OF THE REPTILE WOMAN

It was few days later and nothing so far was heard or seen in public of the reptile shape shifter adult female.

So Abigail happed to be grieving her adopted mother death who was murdered by an intrteder in her home.

So happed to a few weeks after the covid lockdown and her adopted father tim fryler.

Just before heading back to work and Abigail back at school planned to treat his adopted daughter a day trip of the south bank first to the London eye feriest wheel and then to the Tate moderns museum.

So happed to be a very straggle exit dealing with shattered casual balls and baseball bats.

So Mr Fryler and his apotted daughter Abigail take a good glaze at the exit and then Abigail tugs her father to look at twisted hanger washing line and also over two hoarded empty cans of beer on a bed.

So then a woman dressed in a red dressed parches the two of them

Her examples to the two of them she is acting curator of the museum and is glad to show the work jean pitcher at this time of what has been a sorry state for the arts world in general with visters down due to covid lock down..

So Abigail with her appointed father Tim fryler carefully looks at the exebebit and notice a woman drees in summery red drees with red shoes also.

So Abbigail has no idea who this woman is really is as the woman smiles at Mr Fryler.

So the woman speaks to Mr Fryler 'is this your daughter'

Says Rachel miller

So Tim fryler sighs and smiles back at the woman.

'She is mine and my late wife via adoption Abigail is'

'So you bright out to see this elation after the long lockdown due to corvid'

So Abigail gives her father a stone looks to strike grin of with as he faille to mention her mother a passing away murdered by an intruder.

So she says 'sorry to hear that'

So Abbigail is unaare at first that she the female curator of the museum is a reptile shape shifter.

So then a abgials symbiotic necklace starts playing up and she feel a twining scenario on the neck with a small tint humming Nosie and she then rushes of the to the female tilled.

So she heads to the washroom as the computerised voice of the necklace summon her to transmute into microcosmic girl.

'Abbigail time to transmute into microcosmic girl as danger is near'

So she attempts to take the necklace of her neck but it ruses to let do it by telling her 'we must stop shetore as ocne Abigail unit we together my host'

So then she hears Rachel miller heads to the toilet cubical next to her and flung the toilet and then head out and injecting herself with a human skin grower.

So Abigail tip toes on the toilet seat and sees Rachels face change from a reptile lizard woman into looking like a human adult female.

So Abigail gets down of the toilet seat

And then flues the toilet as then she sees the lizard woman termite into having blonde hair and a red flowery dress.

So Abigail gets out of the cubicle and prating she had not seen what has happened Vis the transition shape shifter of the woman none as Rachel miller.

'Hi again Abigail I am just powedering my nose aslo'

So the woman puts a white powder in her nose of sliver foil.

So then she walks out of the female's toilet flowed by Abagail who still at first can't believe what she saw of seeing a shape shying reptile grow skin and her size.

So she Abigail attempts to go in a different diction until her father Tim calls her over as Rachel miller smiles at her father who asks her out for a coffee or drink at the local café or one of the pubs in the embankment.

So she Rachel heads back to the loo and jets herself with a green substance and comes out in a huff of puff with her breathe attiring and felling like devising fire out of her mouth.

So as she talks to Tim and saying yes to him for the date maybe not with his adopted daughter being there next time.

So she yet again heads to the towel and blows flames into the water of toilet bowl.

So then flees the toilet and Abigail gets very succpsisoe of her dads be date to be heading on four occcasions to the toilet in the museum and rising of each time to the Laverty.

So then Abigail takes off her necklace the symbiotic necklace to start off with and places it her pair jean trousers.

But still the home of elite beads of necklace still hums like a huming ecrelticcl generator.

CHAPTER FOUR

THE KICK UNDER THE RESTAURANT DINNER TABLE.

So it was that Mr Fryler invites Rachel miller for a meal at the la Anglia French restaurant to join him and Abigail for bite for a meal.

So the three sit near the of the front of the restaurant outside on a table of four.

So then the wine waiter apaches them and askes Tim frlyer does he want bottler of the house wine a soft drink for the girl.

'What soft drink do you want young lady or shall I say mumrslule'

So Tim orders a merlot French wine and then somehow Abigail seems a bit invited in Rachel but not fully aware if she is a reptile shape shifter.

So as she caches her long hair that's tied in two pony tails her hair being coloured brown.

So then Rachel grins at Abigail who then all of a sudden kicks her father under the table and trying to get his attain as she does not like into seeing her adopted father flirt with Rachel.

So Tim and Rachel tuck into to the starter avocadoes mosses and axial into chesses and ham vollervont.

As the waiter had served them the starters

As then as the tall French waiter series the three main cosies of duck la orange to the three of them in the restraint that's in the south bank a few meters away from waterloo station.

So then she Abigail kicks him Tim her father a second time and he yells due to the hell of her black shoes hitting his leg under the table 'ouch abbey what do you want'

'Let's go dad'

She yells out to Tim who then quits down and attempting not to cause a commotion in restaurant himself by telling of Abigail.

Who then sulks as Tim hands Rachel his bussesinees card as they cell phone numbers and email addresses with her busses card also.

So then she smiles at him and grins at Abigail who stares at her back in anger.

So then Tim hugs Rachel and then Abigail refuses to hug Rachel as then her symbiotic necklace makes a rattling shaking vibrating noise as she touches the necklace in her handbag.

So then Abigail finds herself unable to Comtel her transmutation device in her necklace so then she heads to the ladies toilet and washes her face and then switches of her necklace and her father Tim yells at her.

So then Tim askes for the bill for the three course meal fro the three of them.

So he payes using his Barclays card visa and hands the waiter five pound tip.

So Abigail comes out of the toilet and tugs her father Tim to leave the restaurant she does speak to Rachel as she can't replace mum she says to Tim and looking at her in anger.

CHAPTER FIVE

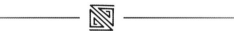

THE JUMP SUIT MERCANCULE NOSE DIVE

So then Abigail stomps her feet in anger as her father Tim walks to the parked car outside the restaurant.

So abbgail gives Rachel a grim anger look as Tim hugs Rachel and he then opens the BMW black car and users in Abigail in with a soft tone of slight anger in his tone of voice.

So then he Tim gets to the driver's seat just as traffic warden is about to put a parking ticket on his car.

So then later on with abbgail being at home she opens her email and sees a new superhero hero costume suit that is coloured purple with also boots that's also clouded purple.

So she responds to the email with photo of the superhero costiumeit that has jet purple back at the back with a mc imrtnal in the blouse like a netball unfrom as she also order ilncluding the intals MC.

So she uses her pocket money debit go daddy card to order the flying the blue flight costume.

so the costume has ability to fly to help Abigail frlyer fly without wings as its is not working due the symbiotic necklace needed to reboot the transforming wingless drive.

So she then sours into the sky above and flies to the city of London were the shared office block and the notices the reptile woman flying with wings toward her.

So the Abigail aliases her superhero self Micrcsomic girl uses her encore lighting rays form her hands top stop shetore form landing on the roof top of the London Hilton metropole hotel in Paddington.

So then shetore at first retorts and then opens her mouth and then flames from her mouth

As which bounces of Micrcsomic girl due having deflector force field in operation activated on.

So then also four police marks men point there rife guns at two of them and then Micrcsomic girl readers and flies of away from the hotel and lands in Hyde park on what happen to hot day a humid day so then Abigail feels something ticking her mind.

so she touches her head felling a voice in her head as she sits on the grass of park unary the one of the men in the park sitting on depth cahier is looking at her with superhero costume clored pink on expert for the mc intalis and then saddle she hears the voice in her head.

so then she heads of home so she does she then notices something.

CHAPTER SIX

THE LOST NECKLACE

So then she then heads of home and not dawning herself as she is in her superhero none self as microcosmic girl and the something with her very seems very strange as she takes of the necklace as the suddenly

She then fined herself transmuted back to her normal self as host of the symbiont.

So she looks at her had mirrow and at spots on her face.

So she looks at the mirror bathroom near the shower unit as she has a change of heart in not at first desiring to wear the symbiotic necklace anymore.

So look at her refection in the marrow and the talks to herself in the mirror 'it will be ok I am sure it will be ok'

So a sound of beam of enjoy happens as the necklace heads into porthole of time with Abigail fryler unearned that someone has stolen it by causing it float into the portal.

So then she heads off to sleep and still a bit jittery

As she hears the voice of Mr Donation a telepath who tells she needs help in stopping shetore the inter world none as draycore of world from race lizard reptile none dryacon.

So it happened to be at school the flowing day she is meet by the telepathic man a new arts teacher at her school none as Manourbroke School for girls.

CHAPTER SEVEN

MR DONNINGTON THE MIND READER ARTS TEACHER

So it was in the arts class that the new arts teacher in the girls school of manourbroke introduces himself.

As class room of 1b in first form sit in the stool like chars on square table that seats fourteen pupils as Mr Donnington writes his name on the flip chart board and askes the class to draw or paint with water paint somethgh they like or don't like that makes them very sacred like spiders of rats to them.

So Abigail happens to be in between Georgina Hayes a fat plump girl with red hair tried in two pony tails.

so next to them in same row is short dark haired girl who is next to Yvonne Mitchel a black girl with long afro hair tats tied back and she puts her up as Alex Donnington the arts teacher asks them who likes to draw an nice adamant like camel or cat or

So then Mr Dondngtion shuts eyes and uses his telepathic powers cases most the class to draw they ether like or dislike.

So then holding a paint brush with green and blue and black paint abbgail draws a picture of a green sally woman witch being posed by lizard woman a dryacon with wings and firing flames form her mouth like a reptile lizard adult female.

So then Mr Donation gets the fright of his life by seeing the pot rate picture of the green teen witch girl and green sally lizard woman with dragon wings blowing flames form her mouth.

So in the portrait the witch of which of resembles jenny maycourt a girl in the school cases Alex Dongtan to freeze with fear also about the lizard woman of which scares him.

So then then says to the class to leave 'class is over accept you Ms Fryler'

So he shakes with fear and looks at the portrait also at Abigail as he looks on the arts Stoll page holder.

Also he tells her about the were bouts of symbiotic nacelle of which has been stolen.

So then a rip in the time qunutunmue happens right away as from shetore who has carted an ad molly in the present due her having an interred key open of time and space.

He tells Abigail.

So she speaks to her the brown heard teacher who has an old tatty brown suite on and then puts the electric kettle on.

'Oh Abigail I can help you find the necklace and also help you follow her in this time but first would like a brew of tea earl gay or regular tea'

So he pours water in to mug and green tea bag other either regular tea or herbal tea like green tea or lemon and ginger tea.

So he others her a few Jacobs java cakes and also a mars bar.

'Abigail nothing beats a nice hot brew he says'

Says Alex Donnington who puts the sheets of large arts papers into an arts paper draw that the class had drawn.

So water the smell woofs the arts room the aura of tea also the smell of water and oil paint and glue in the art room.

So he looks at the partite again of the green witch teen girl and dryacon reptiles' woman with the symbiotic necklace.

'But sir how do I get it back'

'You don't for now'

So she feels a bit upset and he pours another mug of tea and hands her a replicate of the symbiotic necklace a and puts the small battery's in the necklace but it happens to be a prototype and needing a portal drive and as a the orbital drive of inepter galactic portal and defacer force shield.

So he used and says to her ' were it with pride you get hold of market twelve cambric necklace of which three has only been three ever made of the mark twelve so far and the other two are with military commander earth defence of federal cosmic consul of worlds so take care and tell no one of the repackage'

Says Alex Donnington.

Who smiles at her and other her Jaffa cake?

CHAPTER EIGHT

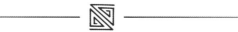

THE FIND OF THE NECKLACE

As then as Abigale sips her herbal tea that a strange Nosie is herd outside the school also the ranting Nosie of a crow bird is herd also.

So then Mr Donnington users she out of arts classroom as the bell rings for the next lesson.

So mostly abbgail can hair the humming nose outside as also Mr Dondngtion.

So with the bell ringing for the next lesson she sneaks out of the school from done satire case and out of the school front gate is metal gate with an intercom for sisters.

So she then walks away from the school gate and feels the power of the symbiotic necklace summers her as it happens to be in a bin outside of the school with cans coke cola and also sweet packets as well summerly stale kababs with flies in the black bin.

So as she puts her hands in the bin and then see sees the necklace with light builds on it and also the median cd shapes power pack computer drive with a single button on it a gay button on standby.

With green amber flashing light so she looks at it and then cuddly she puts the necklace around her neck and the commirerised female voice aces her question.

'it it you a Abigail fryler'

'Yes it's me'

So then computerised female human sounding voice says to her 'is host ready for transmutation'

'A not yet as I have got school and oh I have home economics cookery right now'

So then she heads back in to school via the iron school gates as one of the teacher a slim woman dress in jeans bottoms and truck site jacket as Mrs Rashfort looks at her wearing a necklace.

'Fryler you know the rules about jewellery in class hand to me or I will put you on report or coneveacte until after school'

So as Abigail tries to take it of her neck and hands it to Mrs rash fort the necklace and it dippers and ends up back on Abigail's neck and she tucks the necked under collar of yellow school blouse with also the purple school blazer she has on with purple skirt and tights;

So then Mr Dondngtion apaches to the two them and then uses his telperpatic powered to make Mrs rash fort to lose her memory of seeing Abigail fryler having the symbiotic necklace on her neck.

As she has no idea what just happened and then Alex donation says to Liza rash fort the pottery teacher 'remember tonight is a full moon and you need to be away from the school'

So she yawns and looks at her wrist watch

So Mrs Resort puts on her green hat on hat and then tells Abigail that her better head back in as I hear from Mrs Baxter that is sasaguge rolls you and the rest of the class in 1b are making today.

So then as Abigail thinks for Mr Dondngtion on helping her to recover the symbiotic necklace and looking at her and centring into the school gate and with all the strafe cars in car park and she sees the headache tapping at the window of her office and looking at her watch.

So Mrs Brigs taps again at window o angina and points her hand her write watch the headiness does.

So then Abigail fryler feels a surge of power the symbiotic necklace and the noise a humming noise.

So Mrs Rash fort apaches Mrs Brigs and speaks to her about Abigail being late again for class and if remember she had a necklace I think.

So Mrs Brigs gives a gawky look at Abigail and also Mrs Resort.

'Ha glades what are on about as I can't see her with what necklace'

As and then Mr Donnington use his telepathic power again to make them lose memory of any necklace that abbgail wears.

CHAPTER NINE

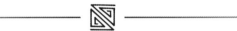

THE HOWL OF THE WEREWOLF WOMAN

So then Abigail takes of her necklace and se meets with Goninan Hayes for the after school club that takes place before the parents' teacher association PTA governors meeting.

So then Mrs rashfort soundly changes into a werewolf and also a strange reptile female woman contents her as the Nosie of howling noise is herd in the school grounds and Abigail goes out to see what is happing and gorgonian Hayes follows her and then all of a sudden.

So then the werewolf woman and the reptile woman turn attrition at the two girls and then the werewolf woman attempts to attack Georgina Hayes and then abbgail tenses into her aisle her superhero self-right and then microcosm girl uses her lightning blue rays to fire at the two of them who both look at each other side by side.

As in the car park outside the school as outside the main building were the main school hall is and the auxllrrery class rooms are on four floors. *Including the ground floor.*

So then the shape shifter changes into looking like gorging Hayes as Abigail pursuits the first wolf woman but not the shape shifter dryacon reptile female.

So the reptile woman takes out a porter electro wand at gorging who then falls asleep and drags goigngina into the back of a white van.

CHAPTER TEN

THE TERROIR OF KIDNAPED GARDENIA HAYES

So then the reptile female shape shifts into her normal self as with scaly green skin and with red swim suite on so then stick out her tong as a fly comes via the van door and gorging gets very scared of what she sees.

So then the reptile shape shifter puts a tape on Gorgonian mouth covering her lips and teeing her to a chair that's connoted to a chain in the van.

So outside the school grounds Abigail looks around to see if the werewolf woman is still around if her friend is of as in being back in the school hall.

so were the parents teachers association meeting is taking place as abbgail hears a racket nose and shattering of a white transit van shaking about as the she sees a teacher appear out of knower who looks like miss woods the English littchure teacher.

So she miss woods looks at the wing marrow of the van as she then looks Abigail who is unary of who is in the van and she apaches miss woods who smiles at her and heads into the main school hall were the PTA meeting is taking place.

as also Abigail update father arrives a bit late parking his BMW car into car park and a bit annoyed at seeing Abigail there and aspic him about seeing a werewolf and her reprinted shape shifter nearby and her friend gorgonian no way to be seen.

So he notes one of teachers as in miss woods come out of the back door of the hall and then disappears and he unary that the blonde hair woman with blue jean suite on shape shifting into being Rachel miller while her users his daughter Abigail to wait in the BMW car.

Then reached rushes up to him and hugs him and very much to annoyance of abbgail but saner she is reprisal shape shifting dryacon lizard woman.

So then Abigail looks at the white transit van and notes a muffled Nosie of a girl crying in the van with also the shaking of the van in the car park area as the moon comes out behind the clouds in this moonlit cloudy night.

So then Abigail heads to the van and then Rachel miller shapes shifts into being a raven as Abigail is fixed on looking at the van as her adopted father tim fryler heads into them main school hall for the parent teacher caseation meeting.

So then the raven bird fly's into a portal wormhole opens in the sky like a wurlpool and then Abigail gets help from the school caretaker Mr Jonson in opening the transit van and they see gorging with black tape on her lips and rope teiid her to a chair.

So it was a few hours later that Abigail fryler sees her friend gorging Hayes who is helped by her and the school caretaker come out of the van.

So the mooring happen after the sleep over and later that she notices that a raven bird has been pursing and even as she gets of the number 46 single deck London bus.

As waving bye to her friend gorging Hayes who happen to sit at the back of the bus on the left hand side next to the window.

CHAPTER ELEVEN

THE DEFFLTER FORCE SEUILD

So Abigail walks away from the single deck bus and she then hears the Nosie above of a revenge bird and she looks up to the cloudless sky blue sky.

Then the bird hurtles in front of her as walks in the pavement of Warrick Avenue.

So she gets taken a back and standing very still as the raven bird shapes shifts into a teen witch girl who looks like jenny maycourt.

So then the teen girl scantly laughs and she and takes out her Elberton portielr wand and types three digits on the nine button flie like wand.

As types she numbers 444 and then as a ray comes out of the wand abbgail frlyer uses her defer force shell from her symbolic necklace to stop the hot red rays from hitting herself from rays form the teen witch as she Abigail happens it be dressed in her school uniform.

So two passer byes walk by as in two men suits with brief cases who glance at eyes at what they see as then the shape shifter transforms into her natural self as a lizard woman who stick puts her tong to capture a fly in flight coming from a dogs pooh from pavement next to a tree.

So then Abigail change from a teen witch shape shifts changes into looking like Abigail's friend gorging Hayes from her class and from school.

So then as Abigail as about to talk to the lizard woman none as shetore she the lizard woman points her left hand into the blue sky and then opens a time portal to a another galaxy into space ship that's a triangle star orbiting a planet like earth.

CHAPTER TWELVE

THE PRIME MEAD CRUSE STAR SHIP

So then Abigail uses her sup hero powers via the necklace to fly without wings into the portal wormhole in sky next to the sun on the right hand side as the black hole opens up next to the sun and Abigail follows pastries and she Abigail fryler transoms self into her alter ego self as microscopic girl the superhero.

So as she enters the wormhole portal and finds herself flying towards as star ship cruse vessel so as she enters the airlock she uses her powers to open the airlock as the space air gushes in.

So then the star ship cruiser is none as the sus prime mead a vessel that circles around the sol our system goring from earth to mars and back also orbing Jupiter also Venus also to the ort region of the glaze and back.

So she is seen on ccv via the star ships security officers who are ordered to capture her for being a store away and having no ticket.

So then Abigail sees a Rachel miler who happens to be bored as the scurry offers try to hold her and then is taken to the lower deck by them of three officers and winked at by Rachel miller how tells a lies to the security staff also the star ship cruiser captain.

Who lets go board after a bitter row with Rachel miller?

So she shows Abigail to on beard luxury bedroom single suite and then uses her conning tracks by placing a orb cube mind probe next to Abigail in the room and then Abigail finds getting first and sleepy and then Rachel shape shifts into her natural lizard female woman self-none as shetore.

So she summons the security staffed as Abigail falls aspen and they put handcuffs on her hands and then take on beard a mine shuttle space plane away from the mother ship of which looks like sea ocean liner with over forty decks and commotion twisty stale areal and windows and an indoor swimming pool on the top deck next to the bridge were crew are icing the captain and helmsman.

So they place her with handcuffs on the back seat of the space plane police shuttle.

So shuttle opens up a wormhole portal and ends up a few light years from earth in the galaxy.

CHAPTER THIRTEEN

THE SPACE PORT

So they take her to the inter galactic space port in alpha centre that is bully on a blue moon with atmespsre in blue dome that has portals and different docking ports with the gates of the dome opening and closing.

So being tied to the chair with handcuffs on she then wakes up and then notes that her necklace is missing so as she wakes she snaps the handcuffs in two and touches her neck to see if the symbiotic necklace is on her neck.

So the security offers attamamts opt to hold her back and then she gets into a tussle as the space shuttle docks into the port door gate arrival bye.

So she's sees all defend type of space ships and the as many them being saucer shaped and heads into the forth terminal building that is very tall and looks like a gray whittle tower block with docking brakes and also in the dome there is flying cars and space time flying taxes that look like new York taxis.

So she runs to the time portal taxied rank area and sees a row of flying taxes parked on the ledge of the terminal building.

So she hails one of the flying yellow cabs as she waits on the meatal path way and looks down at the hover space ships on the river bed of the space port.

So she puts out her hands opt hail time taxied cam with the yellow dot matrix station free for hire.

So the driver a mixed race man says to her 'were young lady In time or space do you want to go as by the way I don't do prehosric ages like dinosaurs in person but back to as early as the battle of waterloo and up to the early to mid-twenty first century corvid second elikzberfion time from 1952 to the Chastain times and more in the future.

So gets on seats at the back as the driver heads out of docking taxi rank port gate and into a time portal.

So ends up in 2021 on Monday 19 July at 4pm in Swiss cottage and haggles for a cheap fare or to payes via her old mobile of which she agrees to accept and ask her for name and current aboard in the time zone.

So she gets out of cab of which parks outside domino pizza in westbound park road and she felling very Hungary and lost in time realises that she has no money on her on anything to barter with as in making a sales purchase for a at least a small to medium sized hawing pizza.

So she then about to enter the domino pizza take away hears a failure noise of something nearby that sounds like an eiearic greater also cracking Nosie of thundering noise of thunder.

CHAPTER FOURTEEN

THE NECKLACE OF POWER

So she moves side way as a tall woman and her partner a man enter the take away pizza restaurant.

So she looks at the bin were the Nosie is come from with also bright light comes from the bin area with very hot air coming from basement area of the pizza take away shop were titre is downstairs flat.

So with metal railings from top of the satire case in Westbourne park road.

So she puts her hands in the black dustbin of which has a rancid smell of stale pizza and empty beer cans and it happen to be evening as rain it pours down.

So she then picks up the power necklace from the bin while as it rains in very heavy in shower downpour.

So then she looks at the power necklace close up with beads of colder light bulld on it and cd like medallion button is immune to the symbiotic necklace so then puts the necklace around her neck.

So as she does she transforms into her hybrid superhero self as microcosmic girl.

So then all of a sudden a portal of time opens up in the satire case.

CHAPTER FIFTEEN

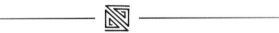

THE RETURN TO THE WORMHOLE OF TIME

So looks she looks ahead to the other side of the portal and sees a triangular space ship docked in ort cosmic city the capital city of the federal cosmic council of worlds.

As of which has an arrival atepshpeshire with lots tower blocks and also Mona rail and flying cars like the moon next to alpha century part from a green dome like none as general space council senate hall.

So the force of the portal pulls her in to the docking port of which she sees a short chubby girl with red hair goring at her and looks a bit like her friend form school none as gorgerin.

So then all of a sudden the red haired girl takes out something from her handbag as she comes out of the space ship as on docking bye landing.

So to the necklace that Abigail is wearing and also the girl taking out a strange object that shaped like cube of metal with light beams on it with six difffrent colours like orange, red. Blue, green, purple, pink and brown that has six sides to it that can be held on a hand.

So she the girl who looks like gorgerin holds the feudal device on her hands as the cube rotated on her hand and then Abigail feels power surge coming out of her aisle her superhero self as Micrcsomic girl with blood coming out of her nose.

CHAPTER SIXTEEN

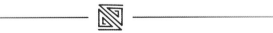

THE FAUNAL DOSE DROP
AND THE ORB CUBE

So then Abigail feels a bit faint as her nose bleeds and four over girls attempt to grab her and take the necklace of the neck.

So then a man looks at the four girls and also Abigail and gorging who takes out form her bag a tube of nose ointment a long tube with a liquid mint smell to it.

So then gorgerin hands it to Abigail but it annoys the four other girls as in jenny maycourt, Vicki Taylor, sandarac banks,philpa hacker.

As the gang of girls from abigal school have trvled in time in pursuit of taking the nackalce of Abigail the symbmbitc mark two power range.

So gorgina hands Abigail a as she puts the fuazal nose drip on her nosrelals to stop the blood from her nose.

So then man who happens to be a frogman fairy general dressed in milerty wear.

also a another man appeaers out of nowere dressed in dark robes and attamts to grab hold of neckalce and out takes a cube like roatateing devive that is a oval crastal ball.

So then as the other man with robes none as empeor zarn summon his men who come out of a portal worm hole of into outside the pizza take away shop.

So the the wizard emoopre zarn fiails ot get hold of it from her and then chants a few words of the orb cube to attment to take the neckalce of the neck of Abigail fryler who is now in her superhero self as mircomsic girl.

So she then looks into the wormhole and sees the tall buldings as in sky scaprers of new York city in the brocklyn distrect like the trump towers and the twin towers before the attack by planes on the two twin towers ofthe world trade centre.

So Abigail frlyer gsapes as she see is a few hours before the planes hit the twin towers.

So looks a few millles away at the commyion of somthigs out of a movie or comic book.

CHAPTER SEVENTEEN

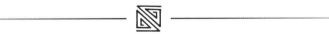

THE WET WALL CRAWLER

So she sees man a coretime that looks like spider man with a all red costume with a sybluble of a spider on his chest as rain falls climing up on the trumptowers and attming to take on a lizrda woman

Who fires flaire of fire from her mouth as she flys in midair.

So she mircomsic girl flys towards spiderman who points to the winged lizarad woman as he attmes to spin a web to knock down from the air on her wings.

So then she Abigail alsie her usprhero self uses her elrtoro powers from her hands to lazer whip lassoue away the lizard who then shape shiftins into a dragon.

So then Abigail uses her powers to use blue lging rays to knock the dragon to blottom of the emprire state blulding and then spider wall crawler thanks microcmisc girl for helping out as the shape shifter retreat.

So also the shape shifter ends intp the wormhole as she has a wormhole portal devive on her and it open to London near the tower of London.

So then a guming nosie happen and the mirocmsic girl finds her self fllaing asleep and waking trapped to a bed abord a space craft hoving orbit and she has tubes fed in her body as well wires all over body unware that she has been adpouted by aliens.

CHAPTER EIGHTEEN

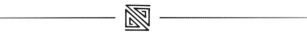

THE MEMORY PROBE

So wakes up and sees room full of dfffent aliens and with one very tall humnosed that's tall and green and also short gray elf aliene beings plus one human man dreesedin white doctors coat.

So she then wakes up and is very scared to see very aline beings around her and she then sees a robtic arm probe into into her skull.

as one of the tall green humanose men ties her and connests wires ino her body and aslo tieing her to the bed with staraps.

so on the bed and one of the alinins a green oval eyes naked aliine swictches on the the arm robitic like probe from a earth like keyboard desk top computer.

So she then tusles with them and then loses her temper as she srtaped to bed abourd the sucer ship vessel in the medical sugery room.

So then she finds herslf falling asleep and ao she gets up in the middle of the night fellin a bit lost and conffesed and then she swtches on the radio to to her favoure radio sation heart fm.

So then she notces in her mind a muming noise and aslo a plsteer in her left arm and heads to lavotry and then looks at her refction on the mirror of the bathroom and then noites that she has pink spots back on her face on the left hand side of her face and a dark mole.

So the huming noise at first upsets unill she hears song by take that the boy band a song called rule the world.

So she then has a vivid flashback and then slups backwards on her bed and falls back to sleep.

CHAPTER NINETEEN

THE SCHOOL GYM HALL FIRE

So waking up on her alarm clock radio she then switches button snooze around and doozs for a few minutes and wakes as also her foster aunt hilda bangs on the door to wake her up and tells her of about having the radio at full blast very loud for time of the day in the morining.

So she heads downstars after getting ready for school.

So she hugs her aunt and gets off to the bus stop in cliffton reoad next to the subway link London tube sation in warrik avunue.

So she waits for the number 46 london bus single deck that takes to her school none as manourbroke girls high school.

So then she hears in her head a buzzing noise and she shakes her head as she attmsts to get rid of the noise as no one on the bus can hear the noise caused by a ecrro chip in her head connneted to the symbiotic necklace she then finds out by herself that she is wearing a loop wire on her collar bone that's made of wire.

So then as bus reches outside of the school gate she sees a lizard woman who then shape shifts into lookog like her friend gorgeina hayes.

So she is one of four who see the the reptile shape shifter change into looking like gorgeina hayes a plump girl with red hair and round spec glasss sroking a white mouse.

So then Abigail gets of the bus stop outside the school and then yells at the plump girl who Abigail thinks in her mind is a shape shifter until her frend gorgeina speaks to her in a calm manour as both of them walk into the school gate.

So then the buzzing noise happae s again and then as the real gorggina hayes turns up and stnds next to her look alikse who happens to be a shape shifter.

. oh which on of you is a reptile lizard chagling'

So then gorgiina stands on the right next to the shape shifter insisde the school gate were the bike sheds are and the main enrtncnce into the school.

So then Abigail shives the two of them to hard conqrete ground and as she shoves them to the ground a power draine comes out of Abigail necaklce as red rays target the shape shifter as the shape shifter drycon female transform back as her self a lizard woman dressed I red swim suite holding a green pole.

So then Abigail uses blue lighning rays from her hands to fire at shetore the shape shifter as she the lizard woman gets of the hard cemnt tare ground insisde the school gronnds were also praked cars are.

So then Abigail ueser her alrto rays to deffend herself with and users gorgina away as the two of them Abigail and the lizrard female duel in battle with phantom blue rays that into very stong chains.

So then Abigail swayimg her red kncoks the rod out of the hands of shetore who then at first reats until she heads towrd the school main gym PE hall and then with a netball training taken place from the six formers shtrore then turns her attention to the school hall.

so then fitthreen school girls in the hall having a PE lesson taken by a short blonde haired woman dreesd in a track suite and nike traners as miss woods who is also the endglish tutor and duputy headmiress hears the commotion outside..

so looking at the window and then all of a suddnen shetroe uses her dragon fire from her mouth to fire at the hall as then flames comes out of the mouth and wings come out of her back of the lizard woman a dryacon.

So then flames cuses the windows of the hall to shatter and then miss woods tells her pupils to avlaute the hall as the hall catehes fire and Abigail as her superhero self microcmsic gilr fails to stop the flams from speading into the rest of the hall as well the school main cordior.

so the staire case as miss woods pressed the fire alamre from the corrdidore were the school tropheys are in cambunts are and photes of past school girls from the school from classes from the four acamdmic hosues.

So then fire biddage are called and aslo the police markmen are summoned also ammberlance crew aslo as seven of the girs suffer from fire smoke inulactcion.

So Abigail frlyer looks on and felling very at first helpless uniil she points the policemarks men to the lizard woman with the red swim suite on aslo with wings.

CHAPTER TWENTY

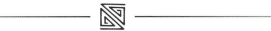

THE ANGRY RACHEL MILLER

So then shtore retreats away from the school gronds and flys with her wings into to a mansion in Highgate west hill were she looks at text message from the aznore emepore zarn resides when on earth and as well as living in the mansion he uses the manshion as a sciecince base also none as the crendore insusuite.

So she is pursued by mircosomic girl in midair as well the royal air force who fire missles at both of them in the sky and then shtorre hurtles downaws outside the gates and pressdd the large red brick mansion and as also mircosmic girl apppches her.

So then abbgial yells at the reprtile woman who in turn gets very angery and slaps Abigail across the face.

'hey supehero girl who do you tnink you are as I will stop you earth girl'

'you wont get away with your fire attack of my school hall' says abgail in anger also and she slaps shotore on her left check on her face.

So then shtrore prssses the intercome videoe phone were the black gates are.

So then gates open as one of the security ghards in the mansion opens the gates but then two secuurty ghards with dobeanon dogs point thire guns at mircomisc girl dressied in her full supeheor costume.

41

So then the two secuirty ghards set the dodmymen pitcher dogs on Abigail who then whliles and the dogs stop growling and says to herslf ' works every time'

So then the sucuirty gahrds take the dogs back in and then a third secourty ghard strarts to open fire vis his pistol gun at mircmisc girl and she uses her force fiels sheld to stop the bulliets hiting her body.

So then she looks at the lizard woman being who then enters into main door by two secoutry ghards into the mansion in Highgate west hill.

So Abigail hears this time a ringing noise in her head and then out of cusirtye looks at sign ouside the mansion a plarck reading in blue the crendore insuitte of scienice.

CHAPTER TWENTY ONE

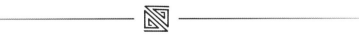

THE ELECTRIC WIRE FENCE

So she Abigail fryler looks up and seesa bob wire with electric wires running thghe the fence to stop intrders from braking into the mansion of which happed to a top scince inststiion dealing with human bioglical symboise studys also emrbroyllge.

So she toche the fence and gets a bit of a shock and then all of a suuddden the rockriler dogs come next to the wired elericric fence with the dog keeper sucuirty ghard.

As the gates of the hosue open to let out one of the scinctist who drive our from the car park outsde of the insteuite house bullding.

So as the dogs Approche Abigail she whisles at thme and the two dogs then lie down with a and whine with fear as Abigail uzseing her cuging trcks to confuse the two rockrilleer dogs.

So then the dog haddlet sucuity ghards sees Abigail standing still and whslting at thr dogs who stop growling with dribble in the mouths and then the rerpiule woman comes out of the bulding holding a lazer whip handle.

So then abigal alsie her supurhero self as micrcosmic girl takes out her portal time stick opner a metal wand like stick with green buld at the end and preses the green button at the tip of the portal wand

So she wlaks into the portal whirlpool and finds herself in hyde park in cenateal London among sun bathers either on the grass or on deph chairs.

So then the reptile womman flollwers her into the portal as Abigail fials to stop her from walking in to the portal and reching at hyde park.

So then another potal opnes with a frogman drsssed in milltery unform who has a cigar on his right hand and a walking stick in his other hand.

So the frogman general none as teloruse solerac of the earth defence league core.

So he noitees Abigail as her suphero self as mircosmic girl and also runing away at the scene in what happe to b a very hot heat wave day as shetore uses her eltero wand to attick abiggial by laze whip.

CHAPTER TWENTY TWO

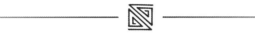

THE FAILED SECOND CAPTURE OF SHETORE

So then four human solders teleorport out of nowere a gun type net deivice and also a man with a shield holdin on his on his right hand who happens to be a supuehero form another deantion none as captail America.

So then liazard woman fires elarcro rays of red beams of slufer red rays from her hands at the four human solders.

so they atttmmt to caprure the evil reptile woman who then flys uowards in a swirls above the six of them linclding the supehero with the shield that has star on it as well as microsmic girl alsiae abigal fryler who trnmsmutes into her supheeo self by presing the buttons her necklace to atttmet to freze the lizard woman in time.

So then shetore flys with her wings into oxford street a few yards away into the west end of London

As buses go thoghe the fameouse stoere past the selffrgeiges depramnt store and dedehmans thire in street as it o in a day with lots of tourists on the pavment were mircoosmic girl.

so she transmutes back to her human self s Abigail fryelr that some how she sees a woman that looks like her late desssced apopted mother pam.

As then who uses blue rays of lightning from both her hands to attmnt to knock shetore down into the ground next marble arch hyde park as soon as marksmen arrive of the police.

also a two teams of supheros from another unuverse coming via two swirling portals as the faill to capuitre the lizrdard female.

CHAPTER TWENTY THREE

THE BATTLE OF OXFORD STREET LONDON

So then out of nowere Abigail finds her self stsnding next to the woman who looks like her mother as she smiles at Abigail outside of the marks and spencer store in oxford street.

'mum it cant be as I thgougt you were dead as you dead in the livening room'

So then Abigail crys tears of joy but suddddly the looklake of her mother shrugs her shloders and to begin with and kises Abigail on both cheeks.

'ok Abigail I have to head to food hall here and what are plans abbey'

So then Abigail points to bus rhoute number 15 london bus and tells the woman who looks like her mother and also speaking like her.

so she then notincg polcice and markmen in teams of four and with look at cctv on the roofs of the stores in oxfrord street as the marksmen look at th footagein vhs cassslte recoder.

So then the woman moves and walks to the left and as she is about ti enter marks and spencer food hall four armed polce others tell her to freze and also Abigail fryle and put there hands up and surrender.

So the woman who looks like pam fryler shape shifts into her lizard like self and then opens her mouth and fires flames from her mouth at the four makrsn men.

so then the senior offers are conated by the mitlary to deploy two fighter jet plains from royal air force to fire bullites at the lizrd femal as soon the reptile woman takes out her anger on civilin personal as in shoppers in oxford steet so a few mintes later four fghter RAF jets atckac the ilzad woman who uses her dragon like to blow very hot flames to fire from her mouth.

so the four jet fighter planses of which all four jets crash into buse road as the street truns into a battelr zone as Abigail fryet tranmsiutes into her superhero self as mircosmic girl as tens of houderds of shoopers icling tourist get injers so then nine poeolple killed poesle due to the conctete falling from budlings of the deepartment stores.

also the four figher jet crasing on the roof tops of the shelfeges as firs balase with bues on fire and also texias and two children aged from five to eigght and girl with a frech accent see thire parernts killed by exdloding buses and cars also taxies from marble arch to oxford sreet.

a yards of bunring verculs and store buldings are on fire and within minuteus soon the emacncey fores turn up as then miricosmic girl mange to uses her powers to knock the reptile woman to the pavment near a burning doeble dcker number seven London bus.

So then insrsted of killing the liezard woman who is bleddimg she mirrcosmic girl hands over to one of the police.

so then paramedic amemclace verslces arrive on the scene also fire brigade as this makes world wide healdline news lincluding sky news and cnn as well as cbs news in the use none by one repoter as the battle of oxrord street on sky news also the bbc news.

'our souces say it's belves to be a alieine reprile being with abillty blow flames from her mouth like a dragon'

Says the repoter of sky news.

CHAPTER TWENTY FOUR

THE CUP OF GREEN GOE

So then the shape sifter transforms her self to look like a police woman firearms officer right in he eyes of abigal fryler who then noitcs that the reptile woman is shape shifter in to human form.

So then a short man with beard appers out of noewere who has horns on his head and hands abigal a cup of green goeey blood into a metal cup with metal handles and he the dwarf docter none as docter wingsly does.

So then abgiial talks to thewith the dwarf doctor by using aline heaing power ot heal the lizard woman.

who happen to have a few cuts on her skin caused by silever blullits and is handed from the police and herslelf to the paramedics.

CHAPTER TWENTY FIVE

THE TRORCHED HOUSE

So then then Abigail fryler opens up a portal with her her portal inter domssnonall rod and then all of a suddedn the reptile woman flollows Abigail frlyer her suphero self as mircosmic girl to were the regntas canal is in maida vale north west London so she Abigail frlyer comes out of the portal hole and coreses thee road and takes looks at the reprtile woman who flowers suit.

So then as Abigail gives her stirn looks of anger the reptile woman holds on her hands a cube like device on hands that swild in glass lavour bottle.

so then she shetroe chants a few wordsl and bolt of yellow rays hit Abigail who lets her force shild down for a few monts and kind of forgets wahts happing for a few mnes as she Abigail walks from small dirve nto her house with her keys to the front door the reptile follwers her in uninvites.

So it was late atefernnon around 4pm with her adoted father tim fryler still at work and aunt and nanny hilda hiaving a bit of a afternoon doze on the cream sofe in the lving room listing the archers on radio four.

So hilda then wakes up form afrn o dose and sees Abigail with raahcel miller who the two of them asin abggial and hilds not raaling that Rachel miller is a shape shifting lizard drayon.

So as hilda takes out Abigail plate of yrsetedays leftover pizza slces with salad so then Abigail comes out with excuse 'aunty I am going to get a darity milk choclate fromt the shop'

So then Rachel tells the two ' I am of to the bank to see about something also getiing book or two from Waterstones in nottin hill.

So then Rachel grins at Abigail and moves to the right as and she Rachel to the left and then all of a sudddnly Rachel shape shifits into a lizard drayocn woman who then dvopours flames form her mouth and the abigal trnsforms via smymbitv neckalce into mircosmic girl via her host Abigail fryler.

So they the two of them sqeuare up to each other with both of them with handson thire hips.

So then as mirrcosmic girl with trnsmauts into superhero trnanume cosmtem in purlpel and yewllow including the cape and boots that are cloured blue with on the chest the symbel leters mc.

So then as mirocmsic girl gets disacted by passeby druken teeengers who leak about as thire is sveen older teen boys from the local pub in madia vale.

So then mircomsic girl punches shetroe the lizard woman on the nose very hard and takes out her lazer whip of which gives out blue rays of lighting of whch raches shrote outsde the smi dechedd house in bollmsbury road.

So then shetore gets very angery altoghe badly hurt then fires hot sulpr rays form her mouth and uses her dragon like flames blowing from her mouithand then shape shfifts in her lizaed nornam slef dressed in red swim suite with red hair and wit her scally skin being green.

So then the flames reach the top landing were the loft is an spaads downsars just as hilds gets out in time as fire reaches all the house at number 23 bloombury road.

So then mircsomic girl askes for her host Abigail frlyer permshion to open portal.

. no no no as the our house its all gone'

Crys out Abigail as she takes out her nackalce and burts inti tears and hands the neckalce ot her aunt hilda just tim frlyer arrives and shouts in saddnes and says oh my goodness what has happed as i have my stuff inside'

So then minstese later the fire bigiade arrive as aslo the amunblance and police and then abigial notches her symitobitc neckalce at the time and forgets her hilda her foster aunt nanny holding to the srtage nackalce that has beads of muite colured small lihght bliulfso nit with aslo a white mdedlion cd type computer devie on her hands as she hilda hands back to Abigail.

CHAPTER TWENTY SIX

THE HOSTEL

So then the police connatact the local socal services regarding Abigail not having a roof I nher head also her apodte father tim who tells the hosng offcer that was as police say was arson causes by a female inrdeer as a statement he says given by his daughter and half sister Hilda.

So then she angly waits at reception in bag packer type of hostel in Bayswater raod west London so as she and father aarive at the repction as short girl with red hair gives Abigail a glariry dirty look with rage on her face as well as the recepnist of the hostel.

a tall slim blulld areb man with a beard who also gives her a dirty look as he at first tells her father how lod is she as the short red girl a teenager aged sixteen shoves Abigail as Abigail and her apopted father stand the front of que.

So then suddly the short girl provkes abigal into a cornftaion as she scqures up to Abigail who then puts her arms on her hips.

So then the red haired girl shoves Abigail and then a tusssel of brawl fight happen as Abigail shoves her back.

So then recopnist behnd the conter aske Abigail to leave the bulding at once or he will phone the police.

So then the fight ends in a fracard as her father gets in row and tussle with the man behnd the conunter also with the red haired girls father who has short cropped hair comated to tim fryler who has gray hair and wearing lesurre wear in form of jogging bottme.

as he aslo t shirt and just holding a rack sack as all most all of his and abgials belongs got burnt in the fire that police and fire inveswrgates see to see if the arson if or not not causes by tim or Abigail his apoted daughter.

So then with two fight breawls taking place Abigail doiceds to back down and tells her father tim.

'dad we better leave and head back to the hosusing depparemnt'

CHAPTER TWENTY SEVEN

THE BEAM AURA OF MIRCCOSMIC GIRL

So then suddleny Abigail frylers neckalce actervates as the red haired girl attmsmts to slap Abigail and pick up a chair to trow at Abigail.

So then a bolt of lighning happens around Abigail fryler and then sybmantint alter ego of the necklace transforms into mircosmic girl dresssd in a blue supehero costume with hair tied back in two pony tails.

So mr fryler is taken aback of what he sees in the reception of were at once saw his dueghter he sees a suphero girl with white glowing hair with also a beam of white glow aronnd her body.

So then superhero girl mircosmic girl looks at the strareld three poeaple in the rectipion area.

So then the red haired short girl takes out from her pocket ortlare elronic wand and points it at mircomsic girl who then atctervates her personal body defflcter shield.

So red rays come from the ortlare wand and the hot red rays bounce of mircosmcis girl.

As the red haired girl none as daffney brakes who with her father ralf also takes out his ortlare wand.

So then the girl and father surge towards mircomsic girl fire rays from thire orrlare wands and then cling thire fists and then mircosmoc girl satands with again with her arms on her hips and takes a bit of a yawn due to realing on her body defefter shield.

So then as two of them the red haired girl and her father combiune thire fractile powers of old fashioned magical chants to try to knock the suphero girl to ot the floor of the reception area of the hostel.

. grim ate low mare' they chant so then mikrocmsic girl the symbiont talks to her host Abigail fryler who wants to sleep.

'not now abbey as we still have work to do as in finding were shetore is she bunrt down our house and made us homeless'

so tim frylers hears abigial voice spaeaking to to the symbaint who has aure and then wodners to himsslk if he is hearing and seeing a permnation or goul with white air and a suprhero outfit on.

so sees his daughter is wearing a smybittic neckalce that marges with his duughter im making into fully into micosmic girl via the host Abigail fryler who gets very angery with symbaint.

'what now you leave me now mircomsic girl or of you don't I will chick the neckalce in the trash bin'

So thnen abibial and her sybmbiant have a qeurrel aaboiut finding shertore the reptile shape shifter.

'I have more chance of finding a new host instead you abbey as it time we merge as one isnstad of qerrling with what to do in puesut of shetore'

So then with anger as Abigail attmpts to take of the symbitiic nackalce and then beam of white aura her body dissparrsas she then succclfully takes of the symbmbitic nackalce and hands it her father.

who sees abigial standing in anger next to the reception who is behind the counnter and she swaying in anger and the the nackalce gets very hot to handle and then mr fryler drops it on the floor due it being bery hot to handle the twenny four light bulp neckalce with also a cd like medaion in the middle of of the gray wire elrtro symbitnc neckalce.

CHAPTER TWENTY EIGHT

THE VELVET SAFETY GLOVE

So then the five of them see the nackalce glowing with a heatwave around the symobtic neckalce and Abigail then speaks to the neckalce symbiont but it indgres her and then she then open up her rack sack and takes out a lead like velvet dark type of gloves and swiches of the non tranmtion green button on the mdaion and then the neckalce cools down and the neckalce speaks to Abigail fryler the host.

'auto ready for transmtion to host Abigail fryler the ontore elve'

So the neckalce floats in the air and warps it self around Abigail frlyes neck the symbiont does.

So then abigial trnanmutes into mirocosmicc girl the symbiont and being merged as one hybred being.

So then Abigail commdans the symbitnat to open a portal of time to Highgate west hill north London to were the crendore scincetfic insuitute is.

So microcmsic girl opens opens the portal neck to the reception area and walks right into the building.

CHAPTER TWENTY NINE

THE MANSION HILLTOP ASSSANINETION

So as she gets out of the portal she sees a fleet of cars and media vans as the prime minster vists the credore insiutte of sincnce on fact finding mission.

so he goes to get a new milrary conatetct with the insiurtte and also the insuitee on that has a small party in calbation of it getting the coantet to make a super pernsal deftecterer shield suite.

So Abigail fryler in her aliease supuehero self as mircomsic girl is usured away from a group of areamed polce offecers.

But until she seses a smiling amircan woman a prees repoter who apppches and askes her what is her name as as superhero.

'well I dunno maybe I am in small fish in gloebal supehero pond with likes of spiderman and supherman I am stuck in microcosm of time and some call me mircsomic girl'

So then the female reppoter from cnn TV heads into the mansion building were the HQ of the crendore science insuirte is basesd in Highgate west hill in Camden north London.

So lots of reporters and police surrrdond the bulding and then the reporter manges to to speak to the prime minster uenare that a rogue fasle police offcer takes out a hand gun from his inside pocket as the prime minster speaks to the report and dances with one of the female sicenitst who has a blue dress on.

So then the cnn femal reporter commmnts on the incation of big scniance brakethgoghe also the reccertion party with mostly strtafe of the insuitee

So then as the prime minster dances with blue dressd womam a gun is fired and then out of the blue mircosmic girl jumps towards the bullet and it defffacts of her and misses the prime mister and then she ducks and then another bullet hits the prime minster on the chest and soon police surround the rogue bogus police offcer.

So then amnlance rush to the scince and then take him the prime misnter to a near by hosrptal in a A and E dpearment and then Abigail fryler alase her supurharo self falls of the dinnin room and she taken to one of the underground labs in the insteutute.

CHAPTER THIRTY

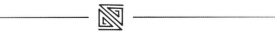

THE ELTORBE DATA DIVICE

So she finds herself in a sicince lab under ground and put into a ultra sound tunnel and the scintst at least four of thme are facasting in the this new type of suphhero who does look like a huaman girl with a symbaintic neckalce.

So then a yong teen boy a student at the insuitere takes a pen like ecienc with a light the end the is clored red and then tunrs to green.

So one of the four scintist logs the data from the elaobe into a main frame computer as she lays semi conssncse in a mild insidced coma.

So then they wake up and tell the sad news of the prime minster colin flitbort smith being killed by a assssine as then as it's a reptialan shape shifter who trnanfoems into a polce offfcer.

So then abigal fryler who trnamustes back as her non suphero self is givne a mapof the glaxey from the future and ilcinclding a poertal know geting to the planet duelore that's forty light years away but a few days away via superlight eaxpader speed.

So then one of the other scintist who has has bald head and dressed like the others in a white overcoat palces a prime into her and he reads the data that realvles she is alien.

So is givne her portal wormhole time and raltivety divce back to her and then transmutes back into her supherro self.

CHAPTER THIRTY ONE

ABGIALS TRIP TO DELROSE CITY

So then she sees space marine genrnal of the unuited fedral comsic council of worlds a frogman none as general solrac dreseds in deesert army unform and speaking with a croake like voice amecan tweang and he hugs her and tells of for miss useing her portal passport to other dommations uniles its used for porper use as in going on a new spying mission.

So he takses he then inverters to the officers mess hall in orbtal creset star base in the moon of sshch as a tall dome like blulding.

So shows a map of a new portal to get to a area of space toward the+ tareuse concalsion were thihre is the main home world of the drycons none better as the lizard poepole.

So he shows a holgrame of the caprtal city of the drarcons main world none as delmore.

'well abbey or shall oi say mc or mircomsic girl I will show to the time portal window on in the top floor before the docking bay of the star ships'

Says the frogman.

So he brings to the window glass portal tunnel and it has water sweril aarond it and he gives a transmtion orb glove of which she shape shftts into lookog like a lizrard female girl,

So goes in the portal tunnel and heads to the other end and sees lots of pryimads and a city monarial and alos flying cars in the red dessrt like city.

So takes out a map of the surreanding area and seeking a a item from a weaponry facrtory as she commmactes with genral solrac the frogman about purching a delta blue sword that cut a lump of rock.

So the city thire is add holowgram posters of candtesd to hwo have enrted the space hunt of time.

So Abigail fryler alise her slef in disguse as a lizrdar girl enters the delmore milrtrety facoryy and shows her badge pass to the security ghard and she is showen to the weapons sho.

on ground floor and give a iinvation to huneter of the race of time of which is a inter glactic tourmant invloing chapons of idie space ship flapsewr palnes foem over eight thossand worlds of council of worlds.

So the secirty gusde hands the iinvation to enter as they unsusre that Abigail is not a lizard girl but in the guise of a lizard girl.

CHAPTER THIRTY TWO

THE HUNTER OF THE RACE

So she is then sohwed to chaging room and puts on space flapper plane gren unforme with on the left hand isde of the top the crest logo of the cosmic coulin of worlds with faetsrs on each side of the planet with moon on each sidw naslo five small stars around the logo crest.

So she is taken to the doking point sation seventeen of the space moter plane port.

So then she nortec that a girl she rgnsesed from school arinves from a pratce run on the flapper space plane of which has flapping wings and is a moden furtsitc kind alternative to a broom stick for wiches and wizrds also elves and fairys.

So then the girl none as jenny mayocurt gets of her flapper space ship and gets out of the space moter ship.

'hey abbgail what brngs you her to demore city asin now a scond gueese shtorte if not me'

Says jenny maycourt the green skiined with with red hair and scals on her face like as she is half liazard she is and ortalre demon.

So then the sound of the halo commnater amosned next to go the practice grind is number four five seven linmore cartford.

So then jenny whioss in her ear lookd at the identy badge of hwic hse has a makeuo flase name on badge.

'it looks like its your turn Abigail and remember to press exlartre and doge the mines and and seek the red space fish'

'ok jen but I never asked to enter this race'

Says Abigail.

. well you must take part or unllls I tell on you as a spy seeking the blue sword of zuse'

So then Abigail goes insie of the flapper moter spart plane and puts her helmit on and is helpme in shtiing the roof of dark sports moter plane with glass roof and has the hemii on with ear plugs and mouth mircphon on her mouth like a kind of plane in the indie space hunt race to bee first to find to red space fish.

So in the city on top level of the grandasrd of the flalpper dockin port thnodnads of pooslw wotich the prativce run of the foulmla flalpper one race.

So then the flag starter man in a boffe dressed in space assounout waves the chekced black and white

Flag so the the lights on a platform tunrs from red to yells and the green for the race star ship race to begin.

So the fifty two flapper space yet planes come of the docking bay holders and then the race commmnater speaks.

As the race starts ' so we both as jet flapper number fourteen takes the lead as the space folrine fish heads into portal space one to credorine the frist out of seven portals in time'

So tweny four flapper deven clarise jhonson heads to the portal and flossed number fifity two piloted by unkown new pilot from earth.

So then one of tial enders puill out of the race due to space dedry in space arnund the orbit so number thrty one princess munrtitys of anzore flapper braks down next to the portal an few mters from portal so then the safty ship arves to r

Ace number eighteen heads into the first portal and miss on catchin the space drone fish'

So then Abigail has a trecker bead on her flapper winged space jet plane from a safety prymid mother ship as well as princes munryits flapper ship.

So then Abigail finds her flapper plane docked in the prymid baye in air lock and she two her suprzie sees a girl with dark hair and green skin dreesd in a flapper space fomuler one cosmume indin a see trew hlemi with a viser on her mouth so she takes of the hlemit as the space airlock doors clooose and she notches Abigail fryler from a previse encounter a few days ago.

So the princess appoches Abigail and out of chacterer for a evil princes hugs Abigail and helps takes of her helmit and visrer.

CHAPTER THIRTY THREE

THE TRUCE OF MUNRYITS

So then Abigail moves away form her after the hug as one of her aides shows her hollograme of a reptile woman shape shfting from a hollgrem cellphone devive as he her perndals adide pints in the middle of the room.

'your royal higness maam and you earth girl this a hollgrmae of shterore we cought on hollograme camra she my ladys is acccding due our igntegance is on a recon misssin in seeking the portal hole number fifty four of the glaxdey leaing to our world.

'what do you mean by our world on a reconsant missinon'

So Abigail takes of her hair band form back of her tied in two pony tails as her blonde hair.

so the tall dark hair man summns munryrits over to take a look at a planet that had one time a civlation with canals and rivers and lots of tower bloakk bulldis and as well lots of greenry like trees as he her homwworld very long ago none as mars or mecore.

so she shows a group of reptile poolse a actervating a superurnaume bome from a space ship on was a planet none as anzore but to humans on earth none as mars now a red barren planet.

So then thee princes crys as she finds out her world was desteryed many centrys ago by the reptialon race of beings none a draycons who plan a invasion to earth and seeking an easy way to earth via using a blended portal space time opener to let a army from a possible invasion to earth.

so then Abigail is also shakes and at first seeim the fact on the hollograme that shortore destred one time the civlation on the planet none now as mars of how lost in the inter glactic war.

So then munrtits the princses looks at Abigail and then she in turn Abigail hugs mumryits the teen princss who askes her aide ingneangen officer to look what can kill a reptile lizard person and mosryly shape shifter as both of them come out of the airlock into the mess hall of the space ship.

So then Abigail is shown ot her seat in the mess hall of whch has large photos of earth past and present supeheros and famosue spys and aslo witich and wizards raging from supepman, spideman to also james bond to also harry potter aslo merlin and aslo the evil villnas in the suphero and magic multiverse

So then Abigail fryler sees a photo of one of herself being none as soon to be the last of supehero magical beings of time none as mircosmic girl.

So then a griup of well wisers take cellphine photos of her from the other part of the mess hall were the longe area is.

So then princess is givne the hollgmrme cell phone of which she shows Abigail again as told by her aide none Darren morgan a afro carrebean bristish man.

'I have a prospale to you a Abigail or shall I say mircosmic girl'

Says the princeess.

'what is it to save your world when its all red as why can I trsut you as you if my host mentions to me via the neckalcce'

'I want a truce in getting back to my first world of was beteful as earth a long time ago as we plan to as in my posole bulld a empire of wolrds in lading a army to take on the dryacon rerilre repbllic of worlds a truce my dear cousin Abigail' 'we aint related jenny as you are bully and I cant change time'

'if you help me by use having clmety truce I will not pick on you anymore and aslo I have in my posssion something that can rip apart a dryacon reptile person.

So while seatin down among the well wiser and aslo munrytits who shows her hollogrmae of a woman holdimng a sword coming out of a river.

CHAPTER THIRTY FOUR

THE BLUE SWORD

So then the Abigail is astonished it what she sees in of lady of the lake holding the exlbure blue colered sword none as the swrord of king arfure.

So then out of nowere in mess hall a gray leather sword holder appears on the table as the is a hollogarme sweitched of.

So then Abigail looks at as the princess takes the sword of the leather gray caseing.

So then she the princess holds the swrord and twists it o nher left hand and looks at her aide and Abigail who gets a bit adajeted and wondering if the princess would use on her but she the princess poseses with sword as the miltrary offers in the mess hall take selfifes photos of her the princess with the blue coulured sword.

So then a thud of noise like thunder is herd with the smell of brew of cemicals is smalt coming via a poral that opens from a witchs coven and all of sudden Abigail finds her self being pulled into the portal of the crndorre casile in decorion city in earthdrol form another univasese.

So four women dreeed in witches black robes souround a clodren pot of whhcih is on open fire with coal and logs with green like goe soup made of funnen leafe and holly.

CHAPTER THIRTY FIVE

THE CLOLSDREN OF FLIGHT

So they giigle with a typcal witch lagghter and look at Abigail.

'sisters shall give the brew of safty flight in seeking

A way back in stoping the nonmags fit of time'

says manever to the three who named deana, colllete and tanya.

So then Abigail panics at first and then one of the wthces in the open forrres next to barn hand her cup of green nettle tea from a small kettle on a nanother fire on logs and coal.

'drink young nomad girl as it will help you to hurturle is shting the vortes rfit if time and make you fly to the open rift on mount sedrace'

'ha ha heee ' the four laghge as Abigail finds herself flyupwards without wings and in the moonlit night in the forest she finds her self unable to contteol her flight with wings as somwhow a portal opens and she wakes up in back of a bus a number forty six London bus arving at warrrick avunue.

CHAPTER THIRTY SIX

THE WEIRD BEHVOUR OF GORGENIANA

So Abigail sits at the back of thw bus next to her friend who looks at Abigail in a weird like look and holding a warrper of a mars bar on her hand and shunts Abigail with a nudge.

'abbey we is the mess hall as you were talking to your self'

So gorggena ratles her arms and takes out a green cloured rabbit from her school bag and offers it a carrot.

So then in a wave of wakening up from a dose Abigail hears the rabbit talking to her frendn goegina and then dancing to to some kind of werird kind of voline music and aslo piano musinc in kind of duo wierd aliine

Music.

So then the other passgers of the bus see the fat plump red haired girl with glasses standing at the back seat area dancing to a sound coming from a metal cordless radiio.

So she dances with rabbit holdin it on her arms and the she tells Abigail ' you missed your stop abbbey'

'in now but you are acting a bit stenange gorgrge'

So in jift of time aabgial finds herslf waking up near the log fire with four witches and the prnceess munrthyits and also her aide sitting around the open fire.

CHAPTER THIRTY SEVEN

THE SCREMING KETTLE

The sisters she has come out of the rift and back her and no skull of the lizard woman here yet via the blue sword of power'

'ha ha this young nonmad is a unown time travler lost in time acding to the tea laafe'

so then Abigail says to the four witchs including the 'sisters lets make her a nice brew of nettle and corrfder tea with rats blood in the potion'

So Abigail feeling very sleepy is givne a metal mug of a kind of green goey tea potion.

so then witchs leaghe with her and also the princes awith her aide as the six of thme drink a very safe potion brew tea.

So then one of the withcs puts masmeilow in in log fire and she heads in her bawn hosue of as she and other wihcs live and smell o cats wee also dead mice smeli in the barn hosue of the three withs in the middle of the forest

So one of the withchs none cafniia heads into the barn and accdntly knoks down crokery and also pots and pans and comes out of the barn.

So she comeso our of the bawn holding a bronze cloured keetle and she then places the kettle on the log and cole other fire and purs blue spicey prtion with aslo rancid mouse blood and the she letd I boil for a few minutes and then the kettle sacmes whe it getd bililed and purs the brew potion in her two sisters cordalliea and casdara.

So she offers the portion to Abigail who rusfes to drink due to wee like small and dead rat smeel comig from barn and then a black cat walks next to the three witches and mows and then crdlaila gives the cat left over of pigeon bird meat.

So Abigail still in slepply mood and ruffssing drnk any of the potion brew due the horrs smell no juse due to the cloudren but also the kettek and the barn of dead rats also cats wee and dogs vomit a real very smelly stach smell.

So then the pricnees akses the three witchs incing her mother corddelaia a tall witch with dakk wae lomg hair who also qween conousr emprees wife of emopre zarn of the anzore empire of dark relams.

So the pricess munrahaits hands the three witches and also Abigail a map atlas of earthdrol the world they in as he gets a call from the emrpeors chife officrs.

CHAPTER THIRTY EIGHT

THE PLAN TO STOP SHERTORE

So he unflolds the five large scrouls of the global atlas map and amother on of pricness aides comes out cia a portal with flash biro borean and sun biro pen at first idededsd himslf and hands over to Duncan as the man that came out of the portal happen to sir douglas maycouurt

'henize so spy hq has noted were and how to stop sherotre your royal higneses and you also Abigail'

'ha ha hee ' the three witch laghe butm not prices and Abigail due the fact shtore in another univesese operated a hbomb on the first home world once ow as anzore prime but no know as mars.

So then the pricnes gives herm other the qweeen a srgne sare as she is drunk on the racid toxi alshoalx brew porion the silver kettle.

'mother its not funny' says the prinesss.

So then her two aunts pot the princes on the back and both laghe our loud due to being drunk and then ducna coghes and as he and the pricnees get very serrse and also Abigail.

so then duglose writes on the biro boear to keys points to stop sherore in andjacnt worlds like earth and mars in stopping the liazard poelsle the drayons from invading earth primeone.

So then the qween dreesed in green robes takes out her wand and makes fire like snake to touch the borad like a hollogema.

'well sisters its to stop her we must use ort power magic' says the princes mumrits.

so then one of the four hands a her roasted rat on a palate with vegtalbes and musroom with rice.

at first abigal rufes ot eat as it has its has rancid of and has an ice smell of turkey aovut that fails drown out the rancd smell of pee.

so Abigail givn int herhugnar pains decesd to eat and then the princess mother the emprees qween deced to paek on beahls of her diaghter munrhgits who is opend lipped and bit upster stil after knowin the wordl in another unvseses was her own at piint but cordialia reshers' anzore is still her and I am sure we can bend time like the last itme'

so the pirnces stoms her broom on the grass ousde and tells her mother and her two aunts aout a paln she foght about.

'what is it dear dughter' says the witch empress qwenn.

so she points at Abigail and says to her mother 'we bait her is in the neckalcw she Abigail wears'

says the princes.

. no no you are not having my neckacle you silly lot'

says Abigail in bit of temper tarni as hs hgtsi n a qweerel with the pricnees as the princes mother the emprrees qween looks and treies her best not to interrupts the qweign two as Abigail says to thep princes ' I wont be idated by or hand my self as fish biait to the reptile shape shifter shetroe'

so then Abigail is haned by a difffentn neckalce but not a symbitc one but a ordanry one.

CHAPTER THIRTY NINE

THE PRINCEPAL NECKALCE

So then the sorrrres queen codrialaia attemts to trow the symbitc neckalce into open log fire until the queens daughter prncees munrtts with backing of the other two witchs stop her from trowi t into the fire as in twst of tussel and gmsnt bteen them all exe avgial agree on handin Abigail a prncpal magcal neckalce isnted of the bronze neckalace.

so then Abigail takes out her portal key and prees four digtits of the nine digit device and then all of a sudden swing gree tuneel is seen a few meters from log fire in the middle of night.

so then she walks into portal inter domashanela tunnes north London were she sees lots of police marksmen outside the crendore accemdmay a bliding that looksl like red bricked eadaction accamtiion.

so then Abigail puts the portiale key into her jean trosussers.

so police marksmen open fire from thire riffle guns at a tall lizard woman.

so the liazard woman is dressed red swimsiute and with aslo red air as part of her scalllsy green body.

so then wings come of her as on the gracvle car park area thire happens to be over seven dead school students.

so then Abigail then fully traforms into her alise superhero self as mircsosmic girl with a red and green costume with red boots and on her chesses thire a large gold star icon on her cheese area so she has hair tied in a pony tail so then mircosmic girl ues her blue lazer whip to laseo the reptile woman with and also uesyin her lazer rays from herh ands to stop the reptile woman from using her red lazer rays at the forteen marksmen.

so the reptile atttmsts to reteat as mircosmic girl lassoes the lizard woman and ties her blue lightning rays around a tree in front garden area of the mansion accemdmey complex.

so then mircosmic girl uses her superehero powers to turne her neckacle into metal.

so then the one of the first ranking officers yells at the retpile woman also to mircosmic girl.

CHAPTER FORTY

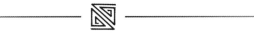

THE ARREST OF THE HILLTOP ASSIGNE

So then the reptile woman takes out from her cllothin outfit a eletcal neckalce devive and she uses a wand like eltrto wand to fire into the air and she then ueses a lazo elteocal rope to cpautre four of the markseman who are taken by suprixe.

so commanded to enter the reception hall of the minsrty of defence crendore insuiuite.

so then the other markmen turn thire atttion on mircosmic girl who then ues her personal defflfrcter shield as the bullts bounce of her and the marekn are very steld as they see blue force shields ray aura aond her body as the bullets bounce of her.

so then on of the offers yell out ' caaze fire'

so then micrcosmic girl enters the reception area and tells the unaremed police men that she will attempt to capture the liazard woman.

'let me get her to you'

so then police reinfencemant markamn follows mircosmic girl to the enarnce of the bullding.

so then mircosmic girl confronts the lizard woman with her blue rays of lihgning from her hands.

so as she does this the laizrd woman shape shiftins into looking like mircosmic girl but then tht real micocmsic girl trnamurs into her into her host self as Abigail fryler.

so then the matkeman are about to open fire until Abigail fryler yells not me I am not a rertile changollg as she is shtotore as that's her name.

so then the marksman fire at first blancs and then live rounds as in silver bullets and then the reptile woman falls to the blue carpeted floor.

so they hold onto her mangange to stop the bleeding with the help of paramedics and then put hand cuffs on her and have her arrested and then palace her into the police van.

CHAPTER FORTY ONE

THE APPPANCE OF THE ORB CAPSULE

So then as she gets out of the police van a long tube like aliine like tube vlecle appats out of noweree that's the size of a small bed with a glaas mirror inti and the rest of the tube like coffin like cube clired in white.

so then four police men hold on ot her and then a medic injects a neddle into her with green flued into her as in like green gow blood supplement.

so then Abigail fryler sllsie her suphero self noricec the time ciuslilce and then as police rush tward her she mircomsic girl sues her her defector sheidl as the ofcers fir rounfd of bullts at her as the over ofecrs get the reptile owlman into the police van.

CHAPTER FORTY TWO

RHE RANGE CONTEOL UNIT
OF THE CAPUSLKE

So then Abigail takes of her pocket in her costume a around cube box wit buttins on it and she holds the beam of cbe with defffernt clours on the plam of her hands as it flsots aboe her hands

so then suddly police then suge forward towrd her and still frin bullts at her and she then uses her gren login rays at thme and stund thmei slow motion.

so then mircomsic girl gets into the time capuke of whuc is coure white and shpe like a coffimn with the letterso and name on it callles nasa time force caouke three thisand.

so she lies down in the capule back down and actws the the time conteler and then trvles a few years back in time.

so she arves in the year 2004 in may in warm humd sping day hmasted heath next one of the ponds of the park.

so then a stange woman isdreded in red dresss walks her dog and troes a stick into pond and the dog chaess after it and fetches it back to the blosnnde haired woman with red dress with a starw hat.

so then Abigail gets out of the capsule as it lands next to the banks of the pond in hamsstead heath.

so then the capsule starts to sink and then suddllnt Abigail srts to swim to the bank side of one of the ponds and gets out of the capsule as it sinks to to the bottolm of pond.

CHAPTER FORTY THREE

THE REAL RACHEL MILLER

So then abigial gets out of the capusilse with scoked clolhtes and seeing woman with hera dog heading towtds the woman with bnnch stick and looking at Abigail whos cloes are very socked.

so the dog shakces the water of it caot and barks at abial an lalso wags its tialigail sees the capiusle sinkin into the btoom of the large pnd.

so she calls out to the red deress woman ' hi its you shetroe ' Abigail says

so then the woman trowns anoter sicj into the pond and looks at the srnge suphero girl and wants to now why she looks like she I abgial now her.

'you are down shtotoe as I wiul use my lazer lihghing rays at you' says abigial.'

'I am sorry but my name is rachel and you are a suuphero as I can see thatby what you are waering'

so then Abigail tkso out the cube from her pokcer and an caes to reractevete the cpauske and makin the cpusle ruse above the waterso then the dog a labosue now as rexmooor swims with its pawa to midleo f thep nd of were the stkc is trwom and then Abigail gets into the water and is hlepd by the wman in getting the capisile of waawswiy from the pond as hse tkss out her dredn puts on her swim suit on.

so then the woman happens to bt a amameuter swimmer in the lido swimming pool in hamstead heath the park from gospel oak side emmnrace of the park.

so she helps Abigail get hold of thr time capsule and tells her ' ypu need to head of home and put some warm cloteso on.'

so then a another woman apro ut of nowere nand hands Abigail a swimmimg cotem and also a swim hat and then disers into mid air.

so then abial then relasie that thewoam with dog is thr real Rachel miller.

and she Abigail then deis a fun swim and then renerts the capsule.

CHAPTER FORTY FOUR

THE CHALLENGE OF THE DRYACON WOMAN

So she Abigail operated the time space capule by preeong the obard buttons on a a blue holograme scrren using her eyes to naavergate.

so she acteses the time capesuel to take her to were the carebouert insetsute is as then she Abigail gets out of the capsule and then sees the dryacon woman using flames from her mouth.

so over ten polcice maeksmen are hurle down to the ground due to indreid heat of hot flmaes and then the shetore the reptile woman cathes in anger mircosmic girl eyes and the offers mirocmsic girl a challenge duel fisght of whits as refoencmnts trun up and hold thire guns at both of them,

so then mircosmic girl acotetes her personal deflter force shield as the reptile woman fires hot flames from her mouth as then sehtore looking at her and the police makenm lagghes and others a challenge to stop her from hurting seven other police markmen outside the mansion of were the crdedore insuite head qeuaters is in Highgate west hill of wich the insuitere is top long tirsmes hill street hole of which has a lng gated masion hosues that keep poelsle out and houses the staftte and stdudnts of the inssuite.

so then mircosmic girl firs up elarclal ca bolts of blue lighnighg form har hands as the the polcemank duck for coever thire plain rght shaelds as then the reprtile woman then tunrs towards the malrkn and then scotsh them with very hot flmaes and four of thme catch fire and then in few momnets two crews of amlance paramdics showc up as then mirocsomc girl aise Abigail fryler tells of the reptile ' you will not hurt the ameclance crew shertoe or will useong supernove super solure freze rays on you'

'ha ha like a typical supeheoro why do you care for thise humans when you are as not even realy human your self'

so then two brave polcice offcers head towards Abigail fryler alsie her suphero self and shvoe her to the ground and then pull out her symbiitc neckalce.

and then as they attempt to put hand cuffs on her wrists she with super powers breakes the the hand cuffs and shoves the two police men to the stone pebbled drive way.

CHAPTER FORTY FIVE

THE PEALRLS OF WISDOM

So then abigial gets up and sees the glance of shotore looking at her aslo the two polcilce offers getong of the gravel stone car park drive.

so then as she gets of the drive she then actevetes her sybmbitc neckalce and then take out her portal inter dimnstion device and a whitlopool of a tunner opens in water llike wormhiel that is coloured blue.

so she then finds herslf fyling into it and then thw offers taken a back by fear and then shotrore pulls out her wings and heads pusring mircosmic girl in to the wormhole.

so she finds hee self a open park green in Paddington London next to the A40 flyover motorway and the local council esasate none as the warrick eastste.

so in the park thire happens to be a few bences and two park keepers huts.

so then anorther wormhole opens as the two pf them sanrd next to the huts as with the noise of traffic comeing from harrow raod, west London.

so a dog a brown laboure is let of its lead by the female owener and the dog wags its tail at Abigail fryler and the grwols at shotroe and then out of nowere Abigail sees a young black teen boy trow a a set of pearls on a chain towards her.

as she the catches it as he tells her to uses to get back in time from the furtre.

so peals has a silver lace sting init with a holes that conet the twenty four peals toegeher.

so the boy comes out of the wormhole and tells Abigail not let shtore have it and also open a another worlhole using the pealrs of widosm that will make her also wise.

none as the peals of wisodom.

so then shorter grisn with grited teetg and scclslaey says to Abigail ' so you want to be become a wise silly suphero with thsese peals as you will surrender to be and also you prince thedore'

so then Abigail as her alsie suphero self puts her arms on her hips and gets very cross with the reptile female adulult'

'you going down shtore ' so then shrotere uses her red lazer whip cords to atmment ot lash mircomsic girl with.

'ha ha ha mirocmsic girl is this al you have by your silly pealrs'

so then mirocmsic girl uses her blue ray of lign bolts to attcke the reptile woman in self defence and stand in front of pricne theordrore.

so then she hands the set of peals ot the pricne thoddore who is also given a portal inter dommshtonal key wand to open a hole in time.

CHAPTER FORTY SIX

THE FLIGHT BACK JOIINLY

So then Abigail frlyer ailase her superhero self follows the prince into the wormhole tunnel and unarre at first that the reprtile woman has puesed them into wormhole portal of time.

so then they head to ardsgarn space port in the planet none as decorionlore in the orion multi sun star system.

so the space port has lots of diffren inter sttel flight vesese from flaeper jet space ships to disc flying sacer space vesels so the space port has lots sliver lamp decking bays that look like street lanetls aslo tower blocks of dedfrent type of space ship pertal bays aslo the space port has forty terrmulals.

so the boy pricne is meet by his aaides ousde the the the royal terminal in port bay four and with his men greting him and looking at Abigail dreesed in superhero alsie self as mirocmsoic girl.

so then they look at the trermanlal dot matcalxe time arrval borard of which reads earth central unvesese fourty minutes the inter royal star ship integraty stping at earth cerntal only.

so themn the comurosesd anoicner says ' the next inter sttler flght is to earth cenatal only onthr royal inrergrry mark four to earthdrol only to area 51 arozna usa.

so one of the princes men buys her a can of super fizz cola and also a tuna mac burger sandwhich.

so then Abigail and thoedore are uanre that the reptile woman is using a pernasl cloaking device to hide herslfe usin a insblble gray inblllebly sheet over her body and as the space craft arvves into the royal trernmal in port five the reprile woman follers them into the space caft that's a ovel like space craft the size of fifty football piches with four wings on four sides of the large oval star ship.

so then Abigail follwes the prince into the royal first class seating passsnger area of the space craft heading to earth cerntal of the milkey way glaxey of the central unvesese of mankind.

so then the prince male butler serves the prince earl gray tea also a plate of cuemaber and tuna sandwich.

CHAPTER FORTY SEVEN

THE LAZER CORD WHIP

So then as the prince is being seved a lot comtion is herd in coridoor and scrames and yells as the nosie of thuder and brght lights red are as the two them look at that cooordor on the the top deck in the space ship cabin.

it was then pricne Theodore is told by two his body ghards as he is about to tuck into his meal of lodester salad that one of them tell him.

'it looks like we have a inrtder on this vessel cusitn havac your royal higness'

so gun bullits are herd also lazer rays of thudlder sizzing noise are herd outsde the royal carrage room and even more yells and secrames'

so then one of the pricnes body ghards takes out a small pistol from his blazer suit pocket and opens the passger door of the space ship seating area and then sees a very angery lizard woman as well as teen girl witch firering rays of red rope cords at each other.

as with solders of the pricne fireing rounds of bullits at the two of them of which bounce of the two of them due to both having deffelter shields.

so many of the solders of the price fall to ground of the space ship corridor dead as as they are hit by rays of the two lazer cord rays also friendly fire from thiire colluges

so then the pricne and Abigail are told stay in the royal passsger suite until the fighting is stopped via the gun bullits and rays.

CHAPTER FORTY EIGHT

THE ATTACK BY MUNRHTYITS

So then as one of the prince body ghards sheidls him from the cross fire he the body ghssrd fall dead on the floor of the royal passgger as then a tell teengge witch with dark jet blck beche hair attmts to attick Abigail fryler ailase mircosmic girl.

so then lizard female woman gives the both of them both thr teen witch girl who happens to bor royal pricnces from a old desset like planet from the past.

so then Abigail fryelr shouts loud at pricnees munrhyits ' hey who side are you on'

so then lizrd woman smirks and grins with griteted teeth and slight giggle of laughter.

'well are have no preface of two of you so far but mybae a truce for the daughter of emperor zarn or maybe not you mun or you superhero girl'

so then the laizrd woman takes out her lazer whip and then mircosmic girl uses her force sheld to stop the lazer from huirh her and then tons of hot fire rays are fired at the princess but she then uses her ortwand then the deflect the hot rays by using a force field also and then munrhits the princes gets angery as she drops her wand and is handed it by pricne thodedore as then in relation munrhetits attcks the lizard woman usieng her ortwand device.

so then Abigail is loked in cross fires as her somwhow her force shield device braeaks down and fells a scoching buring snsasion on her face and stomacche also leg area.

CHAPTER FORTY NINE

THE WURL TIME PORTAL CUBE

So she Abigail uses the sorrsesres princess munrhyits as a shield who has in posssion a eletrowwand.

as well a a elrrocube in a oval crastal ball on a leade ball holder the size of a hand.

so then munrheits hands it to prince thedore who then hands it Abigail fryler mircosmic girl.

so the cube of of different colouirs and numbers from one zero to nine digtal numbrals twits arnd the crastal ball and then a hatch opens on one of sides of the cratal ball as light projcter rays to the side of the royal passgger suite were next Abigail happems ot be standing.

so she sees the wurl inter domamsiton tunnerl as prince theodore eggs her on to head to the wurl tunnel into safety.

as thel izard woman uses her flames from her mouth as she parly transmutes into a dragon and fires at other passssgers in the suite.

so she then purses Abigail fryler micosmic girl int o the wurlpoole blue tunnel that's the clouour of blue sky in a hot cloudless day.

so then as Abigail enters to the end of time wurl time portal the lizard woman then puress her to a canal patheway that's part of the grand union canal in Paddington next to the canlal junction none as little venice were the three canals of the regants canal and Paddington stop as well as the grand union meet.

so it happened to be very hot midweek day as the lizard female adlule takes out her eletrowand again.

so then Abigail uses yet again her deffecter shield as the lizard woman fires red rays of thunder blots from her etlecrowand.

so then as she fires the the lazer rays at Abigail fryler something srange happpes as the repriel laizrd womans type up five dgiters on the flutlel like wand,

CHAPTER FIFTY

THE CHANGING INTO A RAT

So as shetore ues her elecriccal wand for charge power Abigail as alsie superhero self as mircosmic girl avetes at first her personal deflecter shield so then shetore gets cross with her self as well as with mircosmic girl.

so she gives her sanery evil grin with her dark dark teeth so she flys upwrds away from the canal bank side so then lizard woman use her elecroe wand to open a portal but then abigial uses blue rays from her hands and it toches thel lizard who then at first reatrats and hertles down an then next to a narrow canal boat.

so then she shtrore croches down and then shape shitfts into a gray rat.

so she crawls away from Abigail who enters a portal heading to space cruse ship.

so the rat enters the kirchen of space cruse ship none as horizon plus.

so she as well as the rat find themlcves in the corrdore area of the space cruse ship on the forth deck out of ninety decks.

so the star ship resbles a oval with four plane like wings with the magnetic fusion nuclure echshuest at the back cloloreud blue with five fan pulepire armas so as Abigail noitshe she is on a star ship cruswer as well as the rat find themsslves next to fine dinnig room restearunt.

that has swing doors to the kitchen area as well a eanrance to the corriodore.

so then she hears the angry voice of the head chef.

CHAPTER FIFTY ONE

THE CRUSE SPACE SHIP CHEF

So then she hears the very menaing voice of the head chef none a clive underwood a butch man tall and blullt telling of one of his commie chefs.

'claytore who lonn will take to grasp the basics of veg prep like carrots'

so then the teen boy who is a dwarf with a pigs snout and tail as happened to one of race of goyteock dwarves.

so then the chef places more carrots also portaeose un peeled to claytore wniges abouit the work load he has do.

'claytore who long for carrorts as we have party of seventy coming in a hour'

'claytore ' says the heas chef who heads to the kitchen offce to sip a glass of gin and then heads out of his office and then notes Abigail chasing after a rat and then he looks again at Abigail.

'hi thre you yoiung girl cant come in here and were are parents'

so he as well as talllking Abigail yells out to the dwarf boy ' claytore have you done all spuds and carrolts peeld yet' 'no chef'

'claytore how long for veg'

so the dwarfe boy says ' no unnoe chef'

'claytore'

CHAPTER FIFTY TWO

THE OFFCERS MESS HALL

So the head chef turns his atttiion to Abigail and is a bit cross with her enrting his kitchen and not being with her parents.

so then he yell out to claytore yet again by calling his name ' claytore'

'what chef'

'the spuds and the carrots'

'but chef'

'claytore'

so then the head chef clive undewooods usesrs Abigail out of the ktkichen and calls the ships scecurty ghard to take to the brig pf the mess hall as she wont tell me were parents.

so the the head chef notces that the teen boy junior chef accidently cuttong one his finger tips with a knife while cutting the carrots.

'clayotore'

says the very angry head chef.

so Abigail is takne to another part of space ship by a tall mixed race scuurty ghard who rgenses from a newspaper clolume and then takes her to a part of the ship were most ships offcers hand out as in a mess hall.

so then in the miss hall of whc has the smeel of swaty boots an socks aslo of stale pizza from inter space devlery company.

so rancid smeel of semel gets to Abigail as she sits in dinning area with chairs and tables also with portrtes of earth passs a d present leaders as like margete thatcher aslo bill Clinton aslo boris jhonstone.

so as she looks at the poratrs on the well she sees the rat juming on the table and the suddly.

something of whiche startles the the ships offcers as they notice semethnge stgange as in a occcarance.

CHAPTER FIFTY THREE

THE CROW BIRD

So they notce a rat snarling at abigial fryler who then picks up the rat who atttmsts to naw her fingers as Abigail opens a portal back to earth via her ortwand.

so then Abigail finds herself in warrric avune waking from her brisk jonuney to were she lives near from warrick avuenue so gets out of the number forty six London single deck bus waving back to her friend goegiana who is sat the back of the bus next to the window of left hand side.

so gets of the bus near the warrick avunue tube subway sation.

so it happpned to be a very warm day in june with not a cloude in site as in blue sky.

so then the nolsie of a crow bird is herd abouve and then the crow shape shifts into a teen witch girl with a red drees on who then shvoes abigial and takes out her ortwand.

'ok abbey hand me it once'

'who are you anyway to ask for what you want'

'ha ha ha or abbey you don't get it do you'

'na but you look like a girl from my school'

'oh her jenny who is my evil twin'

so then the teen witch girl slaps Abigail across the face and then Abigail slaps and punches her back.

so then the teen witch does a sliding soccer tackle on Abigail and then teen witch shape shifts into back as a crow bird.

CHAPTER FIFTY FOUR

THE INICERDENT AT THE BASEBALL MATCH

it was as Abigail fryler enters into portal unware that the crow bird flown into the portal in time.

that she and the crow find themselves in the USA in new York in the brocklyn disrect n next to sports sadeyum none the yankee sadeyum were a live match is on with crowds cherring and being watch on US TV network channel NBC.

so then Abigail feeling very hungary heads to towards a burger kiosk and she takes out a a USA five doller bank note.

so then the rat seen front of the custmers as being fans of the baseball match.

so the teams who were playing happened to new York Yankees verses LA dodgers part of the baseball world series in fourt match out of the best of seven'

so Abigail hears the live match on a speacker were next to the hotdog koieisk as the owner has thr radio on were the fiidge was on top of it next to a cellphone.

so as the crow shape shifits into back as her lizard self with her wings and moslly saclley skin that's green aslo having red cloure firing eyes.

so then as cheers happen also claps as one of the teams scores a home run.

so then the lizard woman flyupwards abouve the yankee saderyum and hurtles downwards were the players are so as the pircher trows the ball at the batter she lands in front of the batter.

so she then grabs the baseball bat from a short man who is very terrefifed of what's happing so then the the flelding team players yell at the lizard female adult who then opens her mouth and then flames of fire comes out of her mouth.

as the flames hit the battes arms and then polcice as well as ammelance and FBI agents enter the scene as she thatens to scotch every in the satume unlees they arrest a superhero girl who goes on the name as mricosmic girl.

but the marksmen fire theire guns at her but she uses her personal deffleter sheld to stop the bullets hiting her so then opens up a new portal back to London to regents canal in mada vale and this time being pursued by mircosmic girl who then sees the lizard atttming to shape shift back as a rat agian.

but somehow she at frist fails to fully shape shift back and she then sees Abigail fryler asise her alter ego self as mircosmic girl the superhero girl.

CHAPTER FIFTY FIVE

THE MORRING QEKE

So it was Abigail fryler wnt into portal wromholei into the pathway of the rengents canal into maida vale north west London that the rat shape shfits into looking like Abigail fryler as the rat gets onto a moored narrow boat none as the morring quke.

so then the owener of the narrow baot sees two teen girls who a like who get on to the narrow boat.

so then abgol falls down as then the rat shape shifts into her self as a dryacon.

so then the lizrard woman fires flames at the narrow boat even killing the boat owner as the baat catchs fire and then the fire brigade turn up.

so then Abigail wakes in a science lab.

CHAPTER FIFTY SIX

BEARERS OF THE NECKLACE

O she then sees aleiens around her bed like little green men and gray oval ugly looking aliens with also a frogman and one human man putting a wire into her arm and the other being aleine attmet to speake to her about why they sent her aboard the orbital med star ship millions of light years from earth.

so then she wakes up with no memery of being aduted by aliens who as in race green man crated the the symbiotic neckalce for certan humanids to wear as Abigail body as host of the the symbiotic necklace Was rejeeting to the symbkitc necklace due being near a drycon shape shiifter.

so she being woken up sees a brown envelope and reads on the front of the enverlope hand to rghtfull host not a witch ot wizard.

so in the the padded envelopre she sees the neckalce that looks like nothing on earth.

as it tiny light bulbs the the size of a pea with also a small disc computer drve with the pielot light on red as the button happens to be in the middle of the small disc as with chain is a oragmnaic nano worm like scture with metatal wire that's part of the neckalce.

so then Abigail opens her perasnal dairy and then opens a page of ehich reads.

'don't let them do this to you again from your future self Abigail fryler the mircosmic girl spy suphero'

so then a fuzzey drsoey happens to her and she falls down on the carpeted floor in her bedroom.

so she wakes aboiud a large mother ship star ship and like last time she sees alinens all a round her bed as like a hospital bed in a cubical and she cloes her eyes as being very terrified of the aliens.

so they who srarp wires into her and take of the sybmbitc neckalce from her neck and then hand to a teen human girl with dark hair and pale coiasioan skin who wakes up and one of the nine aliens places the nackalce on jenny maycourts neck.

so one of the aliiens says to the group of medics aleina with f rist band on his right wrist with name called fellmore.

he being a little green man.

so then he tells ' maybe we shuild use the mark four symbiotic neckalce on Abigail as she I sure she can bond this time without straming problems as she is showing signs of mutating as a hyrbred so ortmen

lets attmet to make her open her eyes so we can place probe in her eyes as a navagytion devive that's part of the mark four symbiant neckalce.

so they contune to do exmpents while she is fully awake and place wires all her body so she feels sarteld with fear as she cant look at the ugly and evil aliens.

so then feelmore and thr other medics take the wire aprart from a nana liquid elretro water that's cloured blue.

so four others in the space ship hospital ward none as mended earth they have been apduted as well.

so they a sleeping probe into her head via wire that's cloured green and then she wakes up the bench of paddingon green next to harrow road were the laocl police sation is.

CHAPTER FIFTY SEVEN

THE FOILED AGAIN CAPTURE

So then she sees prince paodore and frogman mutant walking toweds as they notice she waking up after being apudted.

so they hand a new neckalce that terlepotrts into he neck as they use a inter active pen to make the neckalce.

get on to neck without her or the boy and the frogman putting the neckalce so she feels a very power surge of power and light rays blue lighting go all round her body.

so she has power tiatuim nano fusion costume that's made from a metal ally that's feels like a metal suit of amour that's cloured purple iccluidong the viaser helmit as she Abigail transmutres into mircosmic green.

so they spake to Abigail fryler about laying a trap for shetore next to a river or canal or motorway verge.

so the the black boy prince is handed a blank A5 sheet of papper and map of west London also a navergation probe of the galaxy.

so it being givnen the frogman mutant human adult male none as genral solrac.

so thep pricne looks at the cellphone like neavgtion cellphone device and sees a blue dot near by a few yards away in the mortorway verge of a roundabout in harrow road west londodn were they croso from heavey traffic as the traffic lights turn to green man.

so they use the neckalce to make themselves very invsble by using the sliver involbluty claak sheet.

so they laye trap of rope with a auto land mine lazer stun gun.

so she smeels the three of them as she gets out of a bush in the roundabout.

so she braks free from the trap and then desrrs the lazer trap device that's connected to the lazer ray stun gun.

so they pull the rope but to no avlile as she the lizard womn retrts by opening up a portal to the furtre in another world.

'abbey take this from me'

so Abigail says to boy pricne ' what is it'

'it's a orbcon wand that can hurt and kill a dryacon'

so they leave the roundabout in harrow road.

so then gernaral slorac hands her a brocure of some kind and also hands a naveygation probe thatsl ike s pen.

CHAPTER FIFTY EIGHT

THE SPACE CADET COMBAT SCHOOL

So it was two days later that genral solrac meets up with Abigail abuuit becoming a space cadet figheter pilot as she shows her dvd of the suucssfull canderdate who joind the space cadet earth defence core.

so happened to be at home while her adopted parents were out at work during the school half term holiday.

so he sits ona sofa chair and sroking her pet cat called Cuthbert and she looks at hime very stangely as she tells the hole truth about shtrore the lisazrd woman being a very advanced mutant from the furtire who is on reconosnse vistin to help lead a invasion to earth bakced by the Mekong mutant apes.

'abgal fryler its time to find sheore befre she leads a large fleet of dryacon star ships to earth as part of a inter galactic war.

'is a shape shiter as I see onec as rat also a crow'

'lets not over play the dramtics as she is very poweeful and a real danger to humanouty in mankind she and her race of dryacons lizard poepole.

so then the frog prince phonee up a jeep to take her and himeslef to RAF moulsfrod a top secret base in north London.

so they wait outside the semi detchesd hosue as the jeep car arrives and she sees two army offcrs who act in a weirf and vlulger sexist way.

'ha you are girl and thire is now way wil cut the mustard' says captail dovea a short haired white male adoult with also mixred race nane as private srowk

so Abigail is helped packing her clotrs and is told by them you wont need them as its cadet uorm all the way.

so she writes a letter to her parenrts of whch reads

'dear mum and dad I have to go on a mission to stop the draycons invading earth I love you mum and dad'

lots of love
abigial

so its at the miritry base that Abigail si shown to one of four doomrryd with bunk beds im them with twenty bunk beds in each dooormntry.

so she happed to beo ne of three girls in the base who had enlisted into cadet space core school.

so the five offer girls happed to be older than her apart from one late teens with one of them being in thire twnetys.

so then the dril sarengent lot comes into doormentry 'ladies it time for the first dril exarsze of the day so chop chop and also you new cadet fryler'

so they at first pussups and press-ups and then tug judo coambat training aslo karttee and Abigail then does well in in exasize as well as the combat fighting of judo and kartire.

so it happed to be after the comabat dril class that Abigail is summned to see captain renolyds apart going on her first mission offalcy as part of MI24 that's affted to earth defence part of the united cosmic council of worlds.

'so cadet fryler what do thnk about a fast track apppche in becoming a opratice private space cadet within three weeks'

'I duno sir'

'you must ask for permsion to talk to senior officsrs cadet fryler'

'permsiion to spaeke sir'

'yes cadet fryler what is your opnion on the matter at hand'

she then is handed a dosure A4 darageme exzie sheet aslo aske to wait for the bases hair stylist as he teels her ' for health and saftery rasons you have either cut your hair or have it ribbon pony tail'

'yes sir'

so then feels a new sensation in her mind after meeting with captian.

so she heads out of the base and heads away from the base past the security booth and one of two mirtary offcers who have red caps on thire head with letters on thire chest area of the unform none as MP meaning military police'

'hey cadet were are going'

'I am leaving her right now and you two cant stop me or me being a real superhero'

'you will be court marshelled if you go abosut without leave'

'I kind have to leave not for going in serach someing in my mind'

'ok so you are home sick then;

so abigial looks at her wrist watch and sees in thoutouts of mind a very brght deivice and then falls down on the pavemnen were the scuurtys both is.

CHAPTER FIFTY NINE

THE CUBE OF POWER

So then abigil is taken to the millatrary hosptial unit on the base and wakes and sees the frogman gernaral solrac and a dwrafe boy as well as prince paidore who sits on the chair opppster the frogman with him being on the left hand side of the bed in a private room of the hospital part of the military base.

so within a fraction of a second Abigail frlyer finds her self yet again abourd a space craft cigar shaped star ship.

she wakes up sees very stange woman with matchos brown horns on her head aslo a semi cirle horn connnted ot each other and she having green skin and dressed in white doctors coat.

'were am I'

'you in med cosmic expepess aumberlance and sit sill Abigail as we are takeing back to the base for a further assement to see if you are comabtlble with new minor orb devivce to charge up nano incsets into your symbiont neckalce'

'but miss who are you'

'my name is mirranda and I know of one of techers in your school who sends her greetigns' so then the doectore tells one of the nurses to take the orb cube of the seven pin plug socket and connnted invery to the symbiotic neckalce and then into her neck and sowing on to her clorr bone as she isa very soon ready drink tunac water'

so then has on ward trollsy in a oval glass ball with a cube of six diffents clours as in red, green, yellow,blue,orange and purpuple.

that roated omn all six sided with rays of liging come out of the cubes in the oval shaped glasss ball on a ball like giant egg holder.

so then they put Abigail to sleep giving her genrral assafatic to make her sleep.

so then next day she wakes up feeling on top of the world and in a good mood to head to school after being unare that she has a coil symbitc nackckle connntesd and sown to her cloler bone and she is told by a voice of the sybmtic neckalce a computerised voice.

'Abigail fryler are you ready to transmute into mircosmic girl right now'

'no '

'but Abigail what about your desire to find and stop her the lizard woman once and for all'

'what lizrard and how are you'

'I am a symbaint and I cant exist without you Abigail'

'so what is a symbaint'

'I am half ornaic and half nano elotrbes used for your race of humanouids none as ortelves'

so then Abigail fryler gets ready for school ann picks her schhol hange bag from her room and says goodbye to her mother who is vacume claneing the corrodre downsatrs.

'be good Abigail and if the head achs happed again plase tell the school nurse' 'see you later mum'

so Abigail walks to neae by bus stop in warrick avunune and waits for the number forty six single deck bus to come and having a bit of headaxg as the cube device ort back up vlace heart devie stops for a few sconds and she teels the the symbainat to reboot as its all she remmmbers from her IT classes due having a talking computrsed deivve in her neck and next ot her heart.

so then the bus comes and it arvives at the stop and heads towards the swiss cottage tube area were her school is none as manorbroke high school for girls that was in fitsroy lane.

so as Abigail gets of the bus she sees three girls smokin next to the school were four benches are in a small sqeure that has a bush part of it and four plain trees.

so one of them a leader of the gang of three girls apapche Abigail and then stands in front of her and attmets her in trcks for enrtitng the school main gate enrtacne for pupuls.

ARCDAIA WOODS

So then the ring leadrer none as jenny maycourt who has jet dyed dark black hair and tatoes on her left arm of a snake with her unfrom of pink bllouse and purleple blaxer with skirt the same clouour with white socks and nike traners on.

so the three girls souround Abigail and slap her acorees the face and take tunrs slaping her and takeing selfie photo shoots on thire cellphones.

so as they attempt gto shove her to the ground were the benches are in the squure next to the school a school tecacher none as ms woods to the pulips gets out of her corsa car outside the school were the bushey squeare is next to the car park and sees the commotion of three girls bulling Abigail fryler.

so then heads towards the the three bulling girls and Abigail fryler as they stop slaping her and taking selfie photeos of Abigail.

so the girls with jenny maycourt are sandar banks and vicki yates.

so the techer who is dresdd in jeans plus aso with a sports track suit top on a addis sports jacket and also puma trrainers on appsches the the three girls and users them away and tells the three of them that will be put on report amnd may by susuepaned from school due to bulling at school.

so then jenny says to miss woods ' but miss we are only playing and she enyouys it the slaps'

so then Abigail hugs miss woods with tears on her eyes and then users the three girls to to the headmiress office on bottom landing of the four block school of manourbroke high school for girls.

so she miss woods walks the three girls plus Abigail into the school sectary recpion office and it has a brown door that leads into the headmirres office so then the sectary rings the offce buzzer phone and speaks to mrs brigs as miss woods users the four girls into the headmires office.

'ok arcdia leave it with me as I amk sure its down to her causing mayehem with my ace pupuls'

so then mrs briggs looks at first miss woods and then to Abigail.

'morrine these tthre have been seen by me blulling Abigail'

"so ms fryler tell if its true or have you been bulling the three of them yourself as a little birdy told me you are up to good yourself"

'but moraine jenny and sandy and vikck I have seen in my own two eyes picking on Abigail'

'ok arcdai its ok you leve it to me while I write a report on all four of you and sen letters with you a warning of next time to all of you four and mostly you Abigail a verbal waening from this time'

'but miss'

'don't but me as you a real trouble shooter miss fryler and no more lies again or even crying to miss woods who is my new deputy head and aslo PE techer covung for mrs dunn who is on maanuirty leave right now and one thing don't let me you four in my offce again and do I make my self very clear'

'yes miss' says the three of them but no Abigail who walks out of the head techer office from green chair she was stting on next to jenny and her two freiands.

so then the three girsl leave the head teachers office and walk past abigial who is busy teaking to miss woods about the after school sports school netball and soccer trals also hockey trails.

so then mrs brigs makes sure the girls are around then shape shifts into a reptile lixazra woman and then opens the portal to kitche avourd the inter stettela space shio crusee.

so comes in the walk in fridge via the portal onto the vessel into one of the fourty resturant kitchens so then as she shape shifits into looking like mrs brggs and has a chefs uniform on and then she sees a dwarf boy comeing towards her.

CHAPTER SIXTY ONE

THE SILLY CHEF AND THE REPTILE WOMAN

So they clouded with each other and seen by other chefs who see the fuuny side in a scsatic way.

so then the dwark boy aslk her. hi what are you doing her as we don't usly have vosing guests back of the resryant unless you want a frute cake or mago tart or evne me dong the hopesroch;

so she the shape shofter shskes her had and then the head chef comes and aks her to leave and ticks of claytore for not working and being to tidy and aslo fast.

so she escoted oiut of the kitchen the kticken so then the woman takes out a tisssssue from her brown handbag nd then leaves the ktickn then is puersed by the on board security staffe as thry look on the cctv moniter and notce a shape shifter on board the space cruse ship.

so then they surriend her in the resturant and then grab her as in four sucuiirty hold her and attempt to take her to to the brigg cells.

bur she then opens a portal and into a another part of the space crsue ship as clayore looks on and and acts very silly by taking hold of corekry and spinimng it in the air using his magcal powers via telocmation powers.

so then corkery asi n plaated and sacers and cups shatter on the kitchen floor.

CHAPTER SIXTY TWO

THE SPACE DERDRIS

So it was as clayotr was being given a warning by the head chef that the shape shifter had changed into looking like the head chef who happed tp have red hair and a beard.

so then the shape shifter points her orrelrtoand at the real head chef until mircomsic girl stops the shape shift in her its trcsk who then changes back into its natulrule lizard female adult self.

so then Abigail attme to open up a portal as then the push of the orbit cuases the crew as well as the guests on boeard the cruse space ship to as thethe space cruse ship as the prorobir deivice is damged due to the portel.

it was the space ships life support progravirty devive as thngs fly out into the ship outsde and into the ships dedreis outside as then abigal closes the portal as few of talbes and chars also cuttelry andcrokery make up deberi ousede the cruse space ship.

so then the laizard female adult opens up a prortal and takes up a photo from her bag and shape shifts into looking like a mr doonongton n a school techer from manourbkek school for girls.

CHAPTER SIXTY THREE

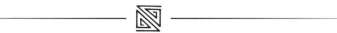

THE SCHOOL WEIRD TEACHER

So then abigial fryler and the other girls from her class as in 1B of the bronte hosue enter the classroom and users them in and then tells them something as he heaeds to the cupboanrd at the back of the arts classroom were the smell of water paint and pesels pens are also blue tuck.

so the arts classroom had four windows and with drawings of trees and anammals on the walls.

so then mr donngton heads to the cuboard were outside thire happen to be a draw of papper.

so he opns up the coboards and sees the real mr doongton tied up in the walk in cuboard tied with rope and hs celler tape on his lips.

so tnen he rugs ar the rope and then shvoes the shape shifter to the floor were the cuboard is and takes out the tape on his lips.

so the real mr donngtion says to the shape shiifter ' you wont get away with it shetore

so then the shape shifter tucks the tape back in the real mr donngiton lips and then places him back on stoll chair and then locks the arts class room walking cuboard that has lots of arts arefets and archive stufv ofrom ex pupuls.

so the shape shifter who is inpersonanity mr doongtion tells the class to leave and do lots and lots of homework.

so the class hears a murming nosie comeing from the cubaords area evn inside so they question the arts teacher and unkown that the arts teceacher is a shape shifter and the real tied up in the copboanrd.

so then the girls head to the coabrs lead by Abigail fryler as she conrfornts the arts techer about who or what is the cuaobaard.

'oh young fryler Abigail it's a dog'

'sir sounds like a person locked by accident in the cupboard sir'

'na na its my cat'

'funny cat human' says gorogina hayes whp satnd behind Abigail her best freaond.

so then the person in the cupaboard brakes free and yells out ' help help me students as I am real mr donngiton as that peron copyin me is a evil shape shifter'

so then Abigail brakes the ciabpard and so then the tenerty girls in the classroom of 1B of first year grade from bronte hosue sees the real arts teacher stublle out of the cupboard as Abigail fryler helps him take out the brown rope out of the chair that's around his legs and arms.

so the shape shifter shows her true to the class as she shape shifts into being her nateule self as a lizard reptile person.

CHAPTER SIXTY FOUR

THE FIRE BLAZE IN THE SCHOOL HALL

So then Abigail frlyer sees as well as the rest of the class scapper out with fear as the lizard woman shape sifter makes her way out of the classroom and heads down the corrdoor to the geonrd floor as the girls run in fear expcet Abigail fryler.

so then she the reptile does a bee turn by truning her head to abigal.

'ha ha ha I regnise you as your alter ego self mircomsic girl'

'na keep her orme out of this as you going down shetore'

sso the Abigail transmute into her supurhero self as mirocomsic girl with a puplle cosmure with letter mc on her chest that looks like a netball uniform and she having puple boots onas well a cape at her back.

so then microcosmic girl trows the first punch of which the shape shifter nose bleeds green blood.

so then the liazard shape sifter loses her cool tempter and then opens her mouth and the blows fire from her mouth into the wall and roof of school main assembley hall on the ground floor.

so then she blows fire at abigal alsie her supurhero self mircosmic girl.

so then the the school main hall gets on fire caused by the reptile woman shape shifter.

so then the shape shifter flys upwards as she the shape shifter leaves the scene of the arson attacj by her.

so then abigal levaes gw hall laso and flys up as she alter ego self as mircomsic girl outside the hall as the school fire almare bell rings and all the school pupls made up of girlsin the school for girls none as manourbroke school girls.

so the girls aretold to stand aay from the hall into the fire meetingpoint as the school techers look at the register and the real mr donngtion nostics that Abigail frlyewr is missing as the fire brgidgda arrive.

so then Abigail pusres her into a alley way in reaing that has the smell of raw fish none as smelly alley due a fishmonger that was thire.

so Abigail seeks to stop as hse flys to the allay without wings at all.

CHAPTER SIXTY FIVE

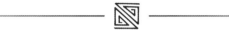

THE CAT ATTACK ON THE REPTILE WOMAN

So then shetore the lizard woman fails to notecice that abigal was pursing her to begin with until all of a sudden abigal sees a ginger tabby cat heading to her jumping from drainage pipe form a cellphone repaire shop in smelly allly central reading.

so then Abigail uses her supurhero powers to cuase the cat to attack the liazard woman by pointing her hands and whilsling.

so the cat sechs in anger and then attcks the lizard woman who then attmsts to shove the ginger cat away.

but the cat retrats after attacking the repailze lizrd shape shifter.

so then the lizard woman shedds a bit of green bloos form her right leg of her thighe.

so then Abigail hides her necklace the real sybitc neckalce in her uner neath her cosmsure blosues and hands the shape shifter something.

CHAPTER SIXTY SIX

THE NOISE OF THE NECKALCE

So then abigial is unwrare of what she has done as she forgets if the neckalce givne to the lizrard woman as a prank to stop her casuing arson attacks is the real one and not realising at frist that the nackalce is with the lizard shape shifter.

so then abgials power as mircomsic girl fade an she becomes her host self as Abigail frlyer.

so then the the shape shifter blows fire form her mouth in smell allaey at her as Abigail runs very fast from the reptile woman shape shifter.

so she rlaes it the flase ocnttefit symbitch nacckalce and has no proeor commamtetin deiice on it.

so then Abigail takes out her tracking deivce from her wrist like watch ans sees that neckcle bing worn is few yards away worn by the lizard woman.

so then abigal hears tne nsoie of the symbic neckalce but them relasss again it's a humming termriop nosie like siren and not of a humming nosie.

CHAPTER SIXTY SEVEN

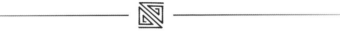

THE FALSE POWER NECKLCE

So then Abigail makes a desssion to summon the symbitc neckalce into making her into chanigning into mircocmic gir the suuphero.

so as she verbl summon the neckalce symbiont ' tramnmute me neckalce into mircosmic girl or locate new wearer'

says Abigail as she then fells no power surge of engey ftom the fake and false symbitcc nackalce.

so then abigial walks into the near by park of ebury park in central reading and sees a woman dnaigng a neckalce on her hands and attming to use the real neckalace true power to cause havo on people every wear as she the lizard shape shifter gives Abigail a stern starre and then shape shifts and this time into a small creature.

CHAPTER SIXTY EIGHT

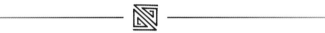

THE CATERPILLAR HUNT

So a group of boys enter the park with fising robs and jars as the lizard woman shape shifts into a catterpilla that's about to change into a craslsle.

so Abigail sees the boys in the park around eight of them invlclingind a boy dred in royal navey robes who is flowed by two grown up men as he the boy a black boy holds a dagger in is hand and then hands it to one of his body ghards.

so the then boys seek the park on the grass of what happed to be a very hot day one june of 2022 a Thursday in hyde park London England.

so the boys plus also the black boy hold a srgenmge a metal ortwand at the grass and then types four digtis of rhe flute like wand and the conrtoos and jolting points to a part of the park were thire happes to a be large tree and he is followed by seven boys and two grown up men.

so they go the hunt for what thite elaertcal instemnets show in the holamorote in the air the shape shifter changing into a caterpillars and one of the boys tells the boy with the red royal robes with afro hair ' that its shetore she I smell is here and also my freienmd the mrocmsic girl lost in time'

so they are told to hunt the shape shifter she is currently in the park as caterpillla.

so they

CHAPTER SIXTY NINE

THE BOY SUPUHERO

So then Abigail notiscs a the black boy with blue royal Robes and long afro hair.

so then he hugs and and then he actevaes his suuphero transfigrion braclet on his arms and then changes into boy with suited red aromour costume and he heads the hunt for shape shiter and very unaawere that the caterpilaere has dispared and he takes out a magnfring class to look on the grass area.

so the pricncs men take out magfing glases from thire robes and onwe of them notces that thire happesn to be a crarrtlsie on the grass were mircosmic girl is.

so then catepillla fials to be stoped in trcacks from shape shoftomng into its natrule self as a lirzard adult female.

so then she the lizard opens the portal in mid air and then all of sudden somethinga not narmal happens.

CHAPTER SEVENTY

THE RUSH OF WIND

So as she opens the portal a very rush of wind runs thoghhe the portal and hevet wind brese as well as blowing wind then sucks them into a diffent world.

that has lots of moumtoms also volcanic moiuntiosn and in the sorindign lots of desserte amnd in the diasstcne lots of forests and on the large plain were the mouuins are incliding are is mount sedrace in the world none as drycore.

so then Abigail as her alse slef a microsmic gril holds on the hands of the black prince none as paidore.

so his hutles into the portal tunnes with his aides of staffe and then lands form the portal into muddy dritch near were a valccano is about to erupt and then they telpporrt out of the way of the volacmnao is to the forssst area is.

so then the repile woman attmts to open a another poral into deep space in orbit of the planet.

so then she sherore thel lizeard woman then blows fire from her mouth in middle of the forst were the pricne is with aides also Abigail fryler.

so as she is about to blow flames at the pricne and his scuirty staffe and then all of a sudden.

CHAPTER SEVENTY ONE

THE FIRE DEFFLCTOR SHIELD

So then Abigail gets very angry with the lizrd woman and yells at her in anger and says to her.

'not today shetore as you are gowing down and you are no match for my defffectore sheild'

so abigial alsie her later ego self sus her persanl deffferte shild to stop the flames from hittinmg her and man and boys also the boy prince who is flambatsted and found powers of mircosmic girl.

so she mirocmsic girl stands infront of them and uses her shield to defend the group of o boys and men also the boy prince.

CHAPTER SEVENTY TWO

THE KINDRED BOY PRINCE

So the boy pricne takes out from his robes a ionvation to attend his father the tribal king of fayemmorac in the planet of decolria.

so then the she when givne it by the good looking blaxk boy prince.

so it a few days as the sstand of with the laizrd woman conntune to happen as then the boys pricne hand him a hand held blue cellpuephone device as he hears his father the tribal king alfont on the other side of the phone at the other end the kings aides as in advicers also the kings best freeind none king ramjax from cranbynoint who is handed the the cellppur from king alfornt.

'my kidrid friend godson padore any lick in stopping the evell lizard woman who wants to do she done to mars centees ago in soulare styetem of earth mankind'

'we are holding tight and may need reonfeonces and tell my father that Abigail is here tryin her very best to stop shotre befoe its to late' so then then laizrd woman then uses oneo her devices and then Abigail and aides of the prince are taken a back'

so then the king ramjax speaks to his kidred boy pricne godson.

'is she still at large as I can see with my satalite cctv screen on my watch my kndred freaind so of alfont the great'

says king ramjax to his godson.

CHAPTER SEVENTY THREE

THE TUG WITH THE DRYCON WOMAN

So then sheotore the drycon shape shifter then uses her rope like lazer ray at mirocmisc girl.

so then Abigail uses her personal deffectore shield as the lazwer red whip warps around Abigail fryler alsie her alter ego self as superhero self mircosmkic girl.

so a tug of power with the hot lazer rope happens beteen the two of them.

so then Abigail tris her hardest to get the to pull the lazer rope of the lizard woman.

so then the lizard woman gives into being beaten in the lazer tug of war.

CHAPTER SEVENTY FOUR

THE BOLT OF LIGHTING FROM THE NACKALCE

So then Abigail gasps for fresh air due ot the insrty of hot fire rays form the lizard womans mouth also the volcanic eruption very near by with fire and brinestone.

so then the lizard woman attsmts to blow fire from her mouth and then all of a sudden mirocmsic girl acteces her challenge bolt of lightining that comes from her body into were the lizard woman is standing just as the volncna explodes.

so then the lizard woman a bit taken a back by the elrtic shock from the bolt of lighting rays decess to use her her main weaponry from her mouth.

CHAPTER SEVENTY FIVE

THE FIRE RAYS

So then Abigail block her defffcro shield but fials to stop her from blowing flams into four of princes scuoruty men.

who fall down dead due the hto fire rays from the lizard woman.

so then Abigail looks at the prince who loocks very flusrared and depply saddned the death of four of his starefe.

so then lizard woman attms to blow fire flames at the yoiung black teen prince but fails as mircosmic girl stends in front of the boy prince.

so then her shield happpns to be about to fail and then out of nowere a portal opens in the forrset as the vloanno does a second ertion so then this time abigial opens a portal to were the boys royal family live inte tribal kingdom of fayemorac in a palace that's has ten storys in it and he and his surrving men land in the court yard as the boy pricne shows her the way of opening and clossoing a portal.

so he shows her to his parents the king alfont and consort qween Candice.

so one of the kings milrary adivers teels the kings son avbout a somwthig that was once on earth going back to king arfure in ancnet England so they enter the waepns room that's all sorts of weapns evne moden day guns and misslse lancnhers.

so they dine and then Abigail gets homs sick but the prince and his pranents hand her something like a weapon.

CHAPTER SEVENTY SIX

THE SWORD TO FISNSHE OF SHETORE

So one of the kings aides also a adviser on milltry deffnce looks at Abigail as her alter ego self miocmsic girl as she opens up a portal and uaare that the shetore the lizard woman awaits for outsidew the school gates of manouecks high school for girls.

so Abigail is givne a silver bluesirsh sword givne to by king ramjaxs millary advvers.

so crowds gather outossde the school gate as the laizrd woman holds the school girl pupils in a bond of lazer yellow rope in tght fir of over eghty girls plus nine school teachers.

so then just as Abigail is aobut ot use her own lazer ray powers to wekne the lazer rope one girl not in tied up stairs at Abigail and themn uses her powers to devastate the lazer rope dvicve as jenny maytcourt girns as Abigail but Abigail crnches her fist as then shetroe notches that Abigail laiss her alter ego self as mirocmsic girl hollds along sword on her hand that that makes a humming noise.

so then frogman none as genral soralc of earth deffnce part of cosmic concile of united fedral worlds smiles at Abigail who she regncices and the rertunrs the smill back at the frogman general.

so then the liazd woman takes out a sword from her mouth and then sways her swrd by twsitng it and then also mircomsic girl and then her powers as mrocosmic girl start to fraine and then the lizrd woman hits moirocmsic girl in the lower chest as her force fleld device fails fcor the first time.

so then a BMW black car parks outside the school with Abigail father tim fryler and his new girlfrfrend none as Rachel miller.

so then the crowd decide to egg the suiuphero girl on as the lizard woman blows flames into the air aand then at Rachel miller the real rechel miller who gets badly scorched and then falls to the pavement as she gets out of the car.

so then the green frogman genral yells ' this is the swrord finshe her the shape shifter'

so then the lizard holds the sword aloft at Abigails head and then abialgal blocks her and then gets very angry as she notchs that the real Rachel miller lies dead outside the school gate as amaelcnce and police arrive on the scene so then the tow tusllle with the swords until the liazrad woman drops her sword due to to Abigail knoking it of her.

then all of a sudden Abigail sways her sword at Abigail neck area and then lizard woman falls dead as her head falls of killed with furisity of mirocmsic girl as the head ends up on the pamvemnt out side the school gate just after the lizard woman about to blow hot flames from her mouth into the crowd as Abigail ueses her deffeccter shield to stop the flames from reaching the crowd outside the school gate.

so then abbgail weeps at her dads new girlfriend being burnt to darth by the reptile shape shifter.

so then th crwods see the body of lizard adult female also the head with green salces on itd fourhead.

so then gernal solace brifs the police about the inscident with reparile and a human woman also a new suurphero girl they name microcosmic girl.

so she Abigail heads of home and comfots her father tim and she then is unarre of what happeed to the lizard woman and also who prince paodore is as a rift in time happens.

so at school the flowing day in the dinnig room abigal notces four girls making fun of her due to her having spots on her face left hand side and grorgina hayes telling her ' abbey aslo have still got the nackalce you told me about'

'yes I have it and also I have seen to a evil supervillain shape shifter a reptile lizard ' she whisprs in her freainds left ear.

'thw world is safe for now from shotroe for now that is until next time for next time gorgrge'

says Abigail who then ywans in dinning table in the school hall and wakes up in he bed in her room and opens up portal ot head back in time as whurl pool of light in a tunnelr opens as Abigail uses her ortptalwand.

so she heads into a vortex into another domnasiion.

ABOUT THE AUTHOR

Roy Peters is a trained chef, author of Microcosmic Girl and The Symbiotic Necklace and Realms of Possibilities. Roy lives in Reading, and enjoys music, poetry and sport, particularly soccer.

Printed in the United States
by Baker & Taylor Publisher Services